The Mystery of the Golden Pocket Watch

The Exciting Sequel to Island Unknown

Gary Henicke

Gary Henicke

gary@henickebooks.com

ISBN-13: 978-0615660561 (Gary W. Henicke)

ISBN-10: 0615660568

For my parents, Raymond and Glenda.

CONTENTS

Chapter 1   Four Years Later

A lot had changed in the four years since Peter's adventure to Island Unknown. Peter, with the help of his cousin Andrew, had become a respected fisherman in his community. Peter spent so much of his time with his fishing business that he never got around to opening a supply store in his grandfather's old workshop. The years of hauling in nets full of fish had built up his body considerably. He was no longer the short, skinny kid of fifteen who dreamed of being a fisherman. Now, Peter was over six feet tall with a muscular frame.

Peter often thought of his trip to Island Unknown, particularly when there were thunderstorms. This reminded him of the severe storm he encountered on the way to Island Unknown. Peter's dog, Captain, died about a year after he returned from the island. He was glad that he had that time to work with his dog alongside him. Peter sorely wished that Grandpa would have lived to see him find Island Unknown. He often imagined what it would have been like to sail home after a hard day's work of fishing and find his grandfather waiting for him on the front porch.

But things were different now. Peter was a businessman and an adult with responsibilities. He and Andrew sold their daily catches to Arthur Milton, the area's largest supplier of smoked seafood. All was well in Peter's life. Andrew was like a brother to him, and Peter and his mother never got along better. Andrew's mother lived with them in Brunswick for a few weeks and then got homesick for Savannah. She had a cousin's children help with her farm there. Peter's family had plenty of money with the gold from Island Unknown and from his fishing business. For the first couple of years people would frequently ask Peter for financial help. Many of them were people Peter did not even know. He tried to spread the word that all the gold was in different banks, but on a few occasions men got into the workshop and searched it for hidden treasure. One time a group of men even came into the house with guns in the middle of the night. They had Peter and his mother sit on the floor while they searched the house for over an hour. Things had settled down now. Peter did help families with emergency needs and he helped pay for a new building for his church.

Peter and Andrew spent their free time with the younger fishermen at the town meeting hall. Much to Peter's surprise, he even had polite conversations with his former enemy, Leech Myers. Myers had mellowed down a great deal since he had given up liquor. He even joined the church that Peter and his family attended. It was almost as big of a news story as Peter finding the treasure on Island Unknown.

<><><><>

Peter and Andrew had just finished delivering their haul of fish to Mr. Milton and were sailing home. They were finished for the week and were looking forward to a couple of days of relaxation.

"Lord I swear we keep catchin' more fish every *week*," Andrew exclaimed.

"I know it. If we keep this up we'll be old Milton's top fishermen," Peter said as he steered the *Free Spirit II* next to their pier.

Andrew jumped onto the pier and Peter threw him the mooring ropes so he could tie up the boat.

"Come on. Let's go see what Mother's made us for supper."

Peter's mother enjoyed listening to Andrew and Peter tell her about their successful catches around the supper table..

"Did anything happen around here while we were out?" Peter asked.

"Nothing around *here*." Mother smiled excitedly. "I did hear from Mrs. Holloway that a new gentleman moved into town. He's going to open up a store. He's all alone with no family. Mrs. Holloway said he's come all the way from *England*."

"Well he must be the man who bought the Emerson's store last week," Andrew stated.

"Let's go into town tomorrow and meet the man," Peter said. "I want to see what he's going to sell in his store."

"If he's a good Christian man, try to talk him into buying John Biddlecombe's place," Mother said. "It's just the right size for a single man. Besides, we need a new neighbor. Mr. Biddlecombe's been dead for almost two years now and that place has become an eyesore what with all the overgrown weeds and all."

After supper, Andrew and Peter went to the town meeting hall to play cards with their friends. The card games were an excuse to catch up on their conversations that they did not have to time to discuss during the week. Peter hated to admit it, but he was there to gossip. He had always disliked the patrons at the Lighthouse Tavern for gossiping, and yet, he himself had become involved. Peter's way of thinking about, and viewing life, had changed as he grew older.

The topic around the card table quickly centered on the town's new merchant. Robert Potter, who worked at the hotel, knew the most about the him.

"The man's name is Richard Brown. I saw it in the register after he checked in. I heard he's gonna sell all sorts of things from England and France, and even *China*."

Peter was intrigued by this newcomer.

"I wonder why a man would come all the way from England and open up a store *here* of all places?"

Nobody had an answer.

The next morning Andrew and Peter cleaned up the Biddlecombe place in hopes that Mr. Brown would like what he saw and decide to buy it. After lunch, they took the wagon into town to meet the Englishman. They instantly spotted the stranger at the Emerson store. He was painting the outside of his new business.

"Hello to you, sir," Peter bellowed.

"Good afternoon young man. Permit me to introduce myself. My name is Richard Brown, and who might you two gentlemen be?"

"I'm Peter Stewart and this is my cousin Andrew Fulton- we're fishermen."

"I thought you might be. Most of the gentlemen in this community seem to be engaged in that profession."

"You really from England? Andrew asked candidly.

Mr. Brown set his paintbrush down. "Yes I am. I come from the city of Liverpool".

"Well, what are you goin' to sell in that store?" Andrew continued.

"Oh, a variety of imported merchandise...furniture, fine clothing, for both the ladies and the gentlemen. Let's see, perfume and scented soaps for the ladies. Things of that nature." Mr. Brown smiled. "I do hope you fine gentlemen will spread the word about my business. It should be open in a few days."

"Oh, everyone in town's been talking about your new store," Peter assured him. "I was told you would be selling things from China?"

"You heard correct, Mr. Stewart. My supplier receives vast amounts of merchandise from the Orient as well as Europe of course."

Andrew was feeling too impatient to go on with the small talk.

"What church are you gonna go to Mr. Brown?" Andrew asked bluntly.

Mr. Brown chuckled at Andrew's boldness.

"Well, I will be having dinner at Pastor Foster's home this evening. I will be attending his church."

"Well, Reverend Foster is *our* preacher," Peter said proudly. "I've known him all my life."

Andrew gave Peter a look. He realized that he wanted him to get Mr. Brown to look at the Biddlecombe place.

"Ah, Mr. Brown? Have you looked for a place to live?" Peter asked.

"No, I planned to search for a home after the store opened. Do you gentlemen know of a house for sell?"

Andrew and Peter looked at each other and grinned.

Peter motioned for Mr. Brown to climb into the wagon and the three of them drove to the Biddlecombe place. Brown was pleased with the house. He was especially glad that it was close to the river. Mr. Brown looked across the way to Peter's house.

"A ship is due to arrive soon with new merchandise. I'll be in quite a dilemma without a storage building like you have there, Mr. Stewart. "

"You mean the workshop? Peter questioned."

"Yes. I've been inquiring about renting a bigger building to hold the items from the ship deliveries. You see I'll be bringing in large shipments of furniture and other goods. The store could never hold the bulk of it. It would also be practical to have a warehouse near the shore for unloading."

Peter pondered for a moment.

"How large a ship will bring your merchandise?" Peter inquired.

"The largest will be a clipper, but I expect most of the deliveries will be from a brig."

"Hmm, Grandpa said he built his workshop here because the water was deeper at this part of the river. I know a brig can dock here. I can go out and measure the depth for a clipper. People always ask why our pier is so long. I figured Grandpa built it that way in case the river got low, but maybe he had other ideas. We never use the workshop. I had planned to open a fishing supply store there, but I don't have the time. I might be willing to rent the building to you to use as a warehouse if you should decide to move next to us."

"Oh, splendid." Mr. Brown shook Peter's hand. "Of course I shall pay you a fair price. I would even exchange merchandise from my store for the rent."

"It's a deal then. We can clean out the workshop before you get your next shipment."

Peter and Andrew gave Brown a ride back to his store. They continued to ask him questions about himself.

"It's kind of a long way from the big cities where we are, Mr. Brown," Peter stated. "You think you will get favorable business here?"

"I have faith in the people of this community Mr. Stewart. You see, I come from a family of businessmen. My eldest brother, Charles, came to Philadelphia twelve years ago. He set up a franchise business there through the export company I receive my merchandise from. Five years later my other brother, Henry, opened up a store in Savannah. Now it is my turn to manage my own franchise. This is new and developing territory, but it has potential to grow and prosper."

Andrew patted Brown on the back. "*Savannah?* No kidding? My family has a farm not far from there! That's where I came from before I went to work with Peter."

The three reached the store and piled out of the wagon. Mr. Brown showed Peter and Andrew the changes he would be making to the inside of the store.

"I shall be needing an assistant in a week or two. Someone to operate the store when I'm away. Do you know of anyone who could be trusted with such a responsibility?"

"Well, there's a couple of fellows I know who might do it," Peter said hesitantly. "I'll have to ask around."

"Splendid. You see, I'll be voyaging to England two or three times a year. My brothers and I will be purchasing merchandise from the same company. We will each take turns in personally overseeing the transfer of the shipments."

Peter and Andrew offered to help Brown paint his store, but he declined. They decided to head back home to mend their fishing nets and to tell Mother about their new neighbor.

"He acts kind of strange," Andrew commented.

"Well, he *is* from England you know," Peter said in Brown's defense.

"It's not that. We know a couple of families from England and they act different. That Mr. Brown is real genteel. I think he's a duke, or an earl."

Peter began laughing.

"I think a duke is higher than an earl. Brown's no duke, Andrew. I'll admit he's right proper and all, but he's no nobleman. Besides, he wouldn't be living over here and *painting* a store if he was."

"Well, it might be that he had to leave England and hide. He might have killed somebody."

Again, Peter began laughing.

"You better stop reading those silly books that your mother sends you."

< >< >< >< >

Another work week soon ended for Andrew and Peter. Although they worked long hours, they hardly tired. They both loved what they were doing. Peter and Andrew often talked of the day when they would own several fishing boats and be as successful as their buyer, Mr. Milton.

Peter and Andrew had heard that Mr. Brown's store was now open. They went down to look at it on Saturday afternoon. They were amazed at the fancy and unusual items Mr. Brown had in his store. Brown had their friend, Robert Potter, working for him. Potter stopped dusting the shelves when they walked in.

"You get tired of working at the hotel, Potter?" Andrew asked him.

"I love this here job. Mr. Brown's a fair man. He pays me better wages than the hotel and he don't cuss at me like my old boss did. Did you know Mr. Brown is even gonna let me be in charge of the *whole* store whilst he's away over in England?"

Just then Mr. Brown walked in from the small storage area at the back of the store. He was carrying a lady's hat.

"Well, it's Andrew and Peter. Good afternoon to you gentlemen."

"We heard you opened up your store so we come by to look," Andrew said. "You gettin' a lot of customers?"

Mr. Brown chuckled.

"Yes, yes I am. I have been doing better than I expected. As a matter of fact, my brother Charles should be arriving from England next week to bring a shipment of merchandise."

"We'll have to get my grandfather's old workshop ready the next couple of days so you can use it as a warehouse when your brother arrives."

"Splendid." Brown glanced around his store. "Why don't you fine gentlemen choose something you like. It will be payment for my first month's rent."

Andrew and Peter looked around for awhile and decided on a tablecloth. Mr. Brown helped Robert Potter wrap up the tablecloth as he was still unfamiliar with such deeds.

"You know, that tablecloth comes from the countryside of England. Your mother will enjoy it for years."

Peter thought for a moment.

"Mr. Brown, why don't you have dinner with us after church tomorrow?"

"Oh, I would be *delighted*. It will afford me the opportunity to talk with your mother. I have only chatted with her briefly. She's a very charming lady, Peter."

"That she is, Mr. Brown. We'll see you after church tomorrow."

Peter and Andrew left to visit with their friends at the meeting hall. Again, one of the main topics was Mr. Brown. Andrew kept to his assertion that Brown, "Had to be a duke, or something like that." The whole crowd of men got a good laugh from that. Peter did admit that Brown is a, "Fancy man."

The next day after church Brown rode home with the Stewarts and Andrew.

Brown even helped Mrs. Stewart prepare the meal. This was kind of strange to Peter and Andrew since Mr. Brown was a guest.

"That sure is a fine suit he's got on," Andrew remarked. "I bet a man couldn't find a suit like that even in Philadelphia."

Peter knew that Andrew was referring to his nobleman theory again so he decided to tease him.

"That's *right*. You know, I bet the queen gave him that suit for his birthday."

Andrew frowned at Peter's sarcasm.

After dinner, they all sat in the parlor and talked. Brown was curious about Peter and his mother, particularly, their past.

"Well now, Peter, how long have you been man of this charming household?"

"I guess I *am* the man around here," Peter said while smiling at Andrew. "Oh, a little over four years now. That's when my grandfather passed away. My father was lost at sea when I was young."

"Pity; such a pity. Lost at sea you say? I assume this happened whilst he was out fishing?"

Mrs. Stewart cut in.

"No. He was lost in a storm while he was sailing." She gave a tight smile. "This isn't something we like to talk about Mr. Brown."

"Good Heavens no. You're quite right. I deeply apologize if I offended anyone with my prying."

9

Chapter 2   The Crate

A lot had changed in the four years since Peter's adventure to Island Unknown. Peter, with the help of his cousin Andrew, had become a respected fisherman in his community. Peter spent so much of his time with his fishing business that he never got around to opening a supply store in his grandfather's old workshop. The years of hauling in nets full of fish had built up his body considerably. He was no longer the short, skinny kid of fifteen who dreamed of being a fisherman. Now, Peter was over six feet tall with a muscular frame.

Peter often thought of his trip to Island Unknown, particularly when there were thunderstorms. This reminded him of the severe storm he encountered on the way to Island Unknown. Peter's dog, Captain, died about a year after he returned from the island. He was glad that he had that time to work with his dog alongside him. Peter sorely wished that Grandpa would have lived to see him find Island Unknown. He often imagined what it would have been like to sail home after a hard day's work of fishing and find his grandfather waiting for him on the front porch.

But things were different now. Peter was a businessman and an adult with responsibilities. He and Andrew sold their daily catches to Arthur Milton, the area's largest supplier of smoked seafood. All was well in Peter's life. Andrew was like a brother to him, and Peter and his mother never got along better. Andrew's mother lived with them in Brunswick for a few weeks and then got homesick for Savannah. She had a cousin's children help with her farm there. Peter's family had plenty of money with the gold from Island Unknown and from his fishing business. For the first couple of years people would frequently ask Peter for financial help. Many of them were people

Peter did not even know. He tried to spread the word that all the gold was in different banks, but on a few occasions men got into the workshop and searched it for hidden treasure. One time a group of men even came into the house with guns in the middle of the night. They had Peter and his mother sit on the floor while they searched the house for over an hour. Things had settled down now. Peter did help families with emergency needs and he helped pay for a new building for his church.

Peter and Andrew spent their free time with the younger fishermen at the town meeting hall. Much to Peter's surprise, he even had polite conversations with his former enemy, Leech Myers. Myers had mellowed down a great deal since he had given up liquor. He even joined the church that Peter and his family attended. It was almost as big of a news story as Peter finding the treasure on Island Unknown.

<><><><><>

Peter and Andrew had just finished delivering their haul of fish to Mr. Milton and were sailing home. They were finished for the week and were looking forward to a couple of days of relaxation.

"Lord I swear we keep catchin' more fish every *week*," Andrew exclaimed.

"I know it. If we keep this up we'll be old Milton's top fishermen," Peter said as he steered the *Free Spirit II* next to their pier.

Andrew jumped onto the pier and Peter threw him the mooring ropes so he could tie up the boat.

"Come on. Let's go see what Mother's made us for supper."

Peter's mother enjoyed listening to Andrew and Peter tell her about their successful catches around the supper table..

"Did anything happen around here while we were out?" Peter asked.

"Nothing around *here*." Mother smiled excitedly. "I did hear from Mrs. Holloway that a new gentleman

11

moved into town. He's going to open up a store. He's all alone with no family. Mrs. Holloway said he's come all the way from *England*."

"Well he must be the man who bought the Emerson's store last week," Andrew stated.

"Let's go into town tomorrow and meet the man," Peter said. "I want to see what he's going to sell in his store."

"If he's a good Christian man, try to talk him into buying John Biddlecombe's place," Mother said. "It's just the right size for a single man. Besides, we need a new neighbor. Mr. Biddlecombe's been dead for almost two years now and that place has become an eyesore what with all the overgrown weeds and all."

After supper, Andrew and Peter went to the town meeting hall to play cards with their friends. The card games were an excuse to catch up on their conversations that they did not have to time to discuss during the week. Peter hated to admit it, but he was there to gossip. He had always disliked the patrons at the Lighthouse Tavern for gossiping, and yet, he himself had become involved. Peter's way of thinking about, and viewing life, had changed as he grew older.

The topic around the card table quickly centered on the town's new merchant. Robert Potter, who worked at the hotel, knew the most about the him.

"The man's name is Richard Brown. I saw it in the register after he checked in. I heard he's gonna sell all sorts of things from England and France, and even *China*."

Peter was intrigued by this newcomer.

"I wonder why a man would come all the way from England and open up a store *here* of all places?"

Nobody had an answer.

The next morning Andrew and Peter cleaned up the Biddlecombe place in hopes that Mr. Brown would like what he saw and decide to buy it. After lunch, they took the wagon into town to meet the Englishman. They instantly spotted the stranger at the

Emerson store. He was painting the outside of his new business.

"Hello to you, sir," Peter bellowed.

"Good afternoon young man. Permit me to introduce myself. My name is Richard Brown, and who might you two gentlemen be?"

"I'm Peter Stewart and this is my cousin Andrew Fulton- we're fishermen."

"I thought you might be. Most of the gentlemen in this community seem to be engaged in that profession."

"You really from England? Andrew asked candidly.

Mr. Brown set his paintbrush down. "Yes I am. I come from the city of Liverpool".

"Well, what are you goin' to sell in that store?" Andrew continued.

"Oh, a variety of imported merchandise...furniture, fine clothing, for both the ladies and the gentlemen. Let's see, perfume and scented soaps for the ladies. Things of that nature." Mr. Brown smiled. "I do hope you fine gentlemen will sprcad the word about my business. It should be open in a few days."

"Oh, everyone in town's been talking about your new store," Peter assured him. "I was told you would be selling things from China?"

"You heard correct, Mr. Stewart. My supplier receives vast amounts of merchandise from the Orient as well as Europe of course."

Andrew was feeling too impatient to go on with the small talk.

"What church are you gonna go to Mr. Brown?" Andrew asked bluntly.

Mr. Brown chuckled at Andrew's boldness.

"Well, I will be having dinner at Pastor Foster's home this evening. I will be attending his church."

"Well, Reverend Foster is *our* preacher," Peter said proudly. "I've known him all my life."

Andrew gave Peter a look. He realized that he wanted him to get Mr. Brown to look at the Biddlecombe place.

"Ah, Mr. Brown? Have you looked for a place to live?" Peter asked.

"No, I planned to search for a home after the store opened. Do you gentlemen know of a house for sell?"

Andrew and Peter looked at each other and grinned.

Peter motioned for Mr. Brown to climb into the wagon and the three of them drove to the Biddlecombe place. Brown was pleased with the house. He was especially glad that it was close to the river. Mr. Brown looked across the way to Peter's house.

"A ship is due to arrive soon with new merchandise. I'll be in quite a dilemma without a storage building like you have there, Mr. Stewart. "

"You mean the workshop? Peter questioned."

"Yes. I've been inquiring about renting a bigger building to hold the items from the ship deliveries. You see I'll be bringing in large shipments of furniture and other goods. The store could never hold the bulk of it. It would also be practical to have a warehouse near the shore for unloading."

Peter pondered for a moment.

"How large a ship will bring your merchandise?" Peter inquired.

"The largest will be a clipper, but I expect most of the deliveries will be from a brig."

"Hmm, Grandpa said he built his workshop here because the water was deeper at this part of the river. I know a brig can dock here. I can go out and measure the depth for a clipper. People always ask why our pier is so long. I figured Grandpa built it that way in case the river got low, but maybe he had other ideas. We never use the workshop. I had planned to open a fishing supply store there, but I don't have the time. I might be willing to rent the building to you to use as a warehouse if you should decide to move next to us."

"Oh, splendid." Mr. Brown shook Peter's hand. "Of course I shall pay you a fair price. I would even exchange merchandise from my store for the rent."

"It's a deal then. We can clean out the workshop before you get your next shipment."

Peter and Andrew gave Brown a ride back to his store. They continued to ask him questions about himself.

"It's kind of a long way from the big cities where we are, Mr. Brown," Peter stated. "You think you will get favorable business here?"

"I have faith in the people of this community Mr. Stewart. You see, I come from a family of businessmen. My eldest brother, Charles, came to Philadelphia twelve years ago. He set up a franchise business there through the export company I receive my merchandise from. Five years later my other brother, Henry, opened up a store in Savannah. Now it is my turn to manage my own franchise. This is new and developing territory, but it has potential to grow and prosper."

Andrew patted Brown on the back. "*Savannah?* No kidding? My family has a farm not far from there! That's where I came from before I went to work with Peter."

The three reached the store and piled out of the wagon. Mr. Brown showed Peter and Andrew the changes he would be making to the inside of the store.

"I shall be needing an assistant in a week or two. Someone to operate the store when I'm away. Do you know of anyone who could be trusted with such a responsibility?"

"Well, there's a couple of fellows I know who might do it," Peter said hesitantly. "I'll have to ask around."

"Splendid. You see, I'll be voyaging to England two or three times a year. My brothers and I will be purchasing merchandise from the same company. We will each take turns in personally overseeing the transfer of the shipments."

Peter and Andrew offered to help Brown paint his store, but he declined. They decided to head back home to mend their fishing nets and to tell Mother about their new neighbor.

"He acts kind of strange," Andrew commented.

"Well, he *is* from England you know," Peter said in Brown's defense.

"It's not that. We know a couple of families from England and they act different. That Mr. Brown is real genteel. I think he's a duke, or an earl."

Peter began laughing.

"I think a duke is higher than an earl. Brown's no duke, Andrew. I'll admit he's right proper and all, but he's no nobleman. Besides, he wouldn't be living over here and *painting* a store if he was."

"Well, it might be that he had to leave England and hide. He might have killed somebody."

Again, Peter began laughing.

"You better stop reading those silly books that your mother sends you."

<><><><>

Another work week soon ended for Andrew and Peter. Although they worked long hours, they hardly tired. They both loved what they were doing. Peter and Andrew often talked of the day when they would own several fishing boats and be as successful as their buyer, Mr. Milton.

Peter and Andrew had heard that Mr. Brown's store was now open. They went down to look at it on Saturday afternoon. They were amazed at the fancy and unusual items Mr. Brown had in his store. Brown had their friend, Robert Potter, working for him. Potter stopped dusting the shelves when they walked in.

"You get tired of working at the hotel, Potter?" Andrew asked him.

"I love this here job. Mr. Brown's a fair man. He pays me better wages than the hotel and he don't cuss at me like my old boss did. Did you know Mr. Brown is even gonna let me be in charge of the *whole* store whilst he's away over in England?"

Just then Mr. Brown walked in from the small storage area at the back of the store. He was carrying a lady's hat.

"Well, it's Andrew and Peter. Good afternoon to you gentlemen."

"We heard you opened up your store so we come by to look," Andrew said. "You gettin' a lot of customers?"

Mr. Brown chuckled.

"Yes, yes I am. I have been doing better than I expected. As a matter of fact, my brother Charles should be arriving from England next week to bring a shipment of merchandise."

"We'll have to get my grandfather's old workshop ready the next couple of days so you can use it as a warehouse when your brother arrives."

"Splendid." Brown glanced around his store. "Why don't you fine gentlemen choose something you like. It will be payment for my first month's rent."

Andrew and Peter looked around for awhile and decided on a tablecloth. Mr. Brown helped Robert Potter wrap up the tablecloth as he was still unfamiliar with such deeds.

"You know, that tablecloth comes from the countryside of England. Your mother will enjoy it for years."

Peter thought for a moment.

"Mr. Brown, why don't you have dinner with us after church tomorrow?"

"Oh, I would be *delighted.* It will afford me the opportunity to talk with your mother. I have only chatted with her briefly. She's a very charming lady, Peter."

"That she is, Mr. Brown. We'll see you after church tomorrow."

17

Peter and Andrew left to visit with their friends at the meeting hall. Again, one of the main topics was Mr. Brown. Andrew kept to his assertion that Brown, "Had to be a duke, or something like that." The whole crowd of men got a good laugh from that. Peter did admit that Brown is a, "Fancy man."

The next day after church Brown rode home with the Stewarts and Andrew.

Brown even helped Mrs. Stewart prepare the meal. This was kind of strange to Peter and Andrew since Mr. Brown was a guest.

"That sure is a fine suit he's got on," Andrew remarked. "I bet a man couldn't find a suit like that even in Philadelphia."

Peter knew that Andrew was referring to his nobleman theory again so he decided to tease him.

"That's *right*. You know, I bet the queen gave him that suit for his birthday."

Andrew frowned at Peter's sarcasm.

After dinner, they all sat in the parlor and talked. Brown was curious about Peter and his mother, particularly, their past.

"Well now, Peter, how long have you been man of this charming household?"

"I guess I *am* the man around here," Peter said while smiling at Andrew. "Oh, a little over four years now. That's when my grandfather passed away. My father was lost at sea when I was young."

"Pity; such a pity. Lost at sea you say? I assume this happened whilst he was out fishing?"

Mrs. Stewart cut in.

"No. He was lost in a storm while he was sailing." She gave a tight smile. "This isn't something we like to talk about Mr. Brown."

"Good Heavens no. You're quite right. I deeply apologize if I offended anyone with my prying."

18

Chapter3 The Sea Voyage

The evening before his big trip, Peter and his mother sat on the porch and talked. He almost told her the real reason he was going to England. Peter knew that his father was one topic that his mother preferred not to talk about.

Peter was excited about the trip to England. He had heard plenty about the country from some of the sailors in town. This whole experience was similar to when Peter left to find Island Unknown. This was an adventure, but Peter was not scared of what he would find; just extremely curious. As they sat on the porch talking a merchant ship came up the river to dock at their pier.

"There's my passage, Mother."

"You be careful out there and do everything Mr. Brown or the captain tells you."

"Yes ma'am. I'm sure they make these crossings pretty regular. Probably see several ships along the way."

"You get a chance you find out who sent the watch."

Peter was taken aback.

"Uh, yes. I can ask Mr. Brown to help."

"Peter, I'm wiser than you think. Don't forget that."

"Yes ma'am you are at that. So, you knew all along why I was going?"

"You come back with some answers, son."

Andrew awakened Peter early the next morning. It was clear that he was anxious to see his family because he was already dressed.

"Hurry up!" he yelled. "The ship must've got here after we went to sleep."

"It got here late in the evening. You were asleep"

Peter slowly got out of bed and started gathering the clothes he would wear.

"I've already eaten breakfast." Andrew looked out the window. "I see the crew moving around on the ship. That means they will be ready to leave soon."

"I guess I'm leaving for England," he said to himself. "At least to Savannah first."

Peter quickly dressed and went into the kitchen. Mother already had his breakfast ready for him. Later, as Peter was gathering up his things, he heard a knock at the door. He looked out the window. It was Mr. Brown.

"Good morning to you, Peter. I know it's ahead of schedule, but are you ready for the voyage?"

"Yes sir. I was just about to start walking to the pier."

Peter and Andrew carried their things out to the pier while Mr. Brown lagged behind to talk with Mrs. Stewart.

Peter handed Andrew and Mother's bags to him on the Free Spirit II.

"Don't get yourself in a hurry," Peter cautioned. "Take good care of my boat."

"Ah, don't worry, cousin. I was only kidding about sailing fast. I know your mother don't like to sail. I'll make it as smooth as I can."

Peter helped his mother on board. He embraced her and she wished him luck.

"Remember what Mr. Thomas down at the bank said," she reminded him.

"I should go by the bank every time I'm in Savannah."

"That's right. It's been a long time since you went there. I wouldn't hurt to bring back some money in case we have an emergency."

Neither Peter nor his mother wanted an emotional farewell. Mr. Brown and Peter walked over to the ship together.

"It's not as big ship as I thought it would be," Peter said as he adjusted his belongings.

Brown laughed.

"No, Peter, The Shiloh it isn't large. This brig is used to transport merchandise along the coast from Nassau to New York. The company's transatlantic ship is waiting for us in Savannah. It's a clipper ship. I think you'll find it to your liking."

Mr. Brown introduced Peter and Andrew to the captain, Nate Chester. Chester could not have been more than five feet tall and one hundred twenty pounds, but he had the voice of a giant.

As they sailed away on The Shiloh, Peter stood on the stern and watched Andrew pilot the Free Spirit II away from the dock. To his surprise Mother was out on deck. Andrew drew up alongside.

"You keep it steady, Captain Fulton," Peter shouted to Andrew.

"Yes sir."

"I won't let him do anything crazy," Mother yelled back.

Andrew slowly lagged a little further behind as they cleared St. Simons Island. He would stay closer to shore for Mother.

Mr. Brown and Peter walked around The Shiloh and watched the crew at work.

"Can you imagine being a captain like that Chester fellow?" Mr. Brown questioned. "He doesn't appear to be much older than you."

"Yeah? I'll admit he doesn't have to do as much heavy lifting as I do when I'm out fishin', but Andrew and I are captains in a way. Besides, we work for ourselves and he works for a company."

Mr. Brown thought for a moment and nodded.

"That's true. I suppose Captain Chester can't take time off like you can."

Peter laughed. "We can't get fired neither."

Later, Captain Chester invited Brown and Peter to have lunch with him below deck. The cook made one of the best meals they had ever eaten. Even Mr. Brown was impressed.

"Yes sir, when men work hard they deserve good food," Chester said. "The Carey Company over in

England always hires good cooks. It makes the men happy and they don't up and quit like deck hands for other companies."

"He's quite right, Peter. The cooks on the transatlantic ships are the finest," Brown said. He turned to Chester. "Captain Chester, whom shall our captain be for our voyage to Liverpool? I noticed Captain Dorsett brought my brother Charles recently."

"I won't be Dorsett. You'll be getting Gibson." Captain Chester looked at Peter. "Mr. Brown? Will you agree with me that John Gibson's the best captain there is?"

Brown nodded enthusiastically.

"Splendid. He was the captain who brought me when I first came over from England. You know, Gibson's great grandfather was one of the first to bring colonists over here."

"How did you get to be captain?" Peter asked.

"I earned it," Chester said bluntly. "I've worked for this company since I was twelve. I figure I got maybe forty or fifty years of sailing left before I die. After a few years, I want to work my way up to transatlantic captain. After that, I want to sail the China route and find some new countries for the company to trade with."

It had been a few years since Peter had been to the Savannah area. It was approaching the evening hours and the lightstation at Tybee Island was glowing. A pilot boat met them and guided them up the river. The river pilot was not too happy about taking them so near to night time, but he changed his attitude when Captain Chester tossed him a small bag of money. When they passed Fort Jackson, Peter could tell the town had grown. People had not yet gone to bed so there were lamps still lit in the houses near the docks.

As soon as the ship was secured, Chester was barking out orders to his men. They began loading up The Shiloh with supplies that were bound for Norfolk, Virginia the next morning.

Mr. Brown went to look for the captain of their transatlantic voyage. Peter walked along the docks to wait for Andrew and Mother.

After a few minutes Andrew brought the Free Spirit II in to the docks. Peter helped moor it to the dock and help mother out.

They were was amazed at the amount of tobacco stacked up everywhere. A few minutes later, Brown came back with another man. It was pretty obvious to them and that he was Brown's brother since they looked so much alike.

"Gentlemen, and lady, I'd like to introduce my brother, Henry."

"Pleasure to meet all of you," Henry said as he bowed his head. "Richard was just telling me that one of you lives outside of town."

"That'd be me," Andrew answered. "I live about ten miles away. The Fulton farm?

Henry shook his head.

"It's near the Lumley's plantation."

"Oh, yes," Henry said. "Mrs. Lumley has purchased several things from my store. As a matter of fact she ordered some items that you and Richard will be bringing back with you."

"The Fulton farm belongs to my sister," Mother added.

"Well, a fellow Savannah resident. It's nearly dark. I would be delighted to have you all join my brother and stay the night with my family. You can then sail to your home in the morning."

"You Browns sure are friendly people," Andrew said. "This has been a good trip. I ain't had to spend *no* money."

The next morning Peter, Mother and Andrew said their good-byes once again as Andrew headed up the river with Mother to his home.

Mr. Brown directed Peter to their ship, The Confidence. As promised by Brown, Peter was impressed with the large clipper ship. They went on board and down to the captain's quarters.

Captain Gibson was just about the biggest man Peter had ever seen. He had to duck and turn sideways to fit through the doorways. To his surprise, Gibson was also one of the most likable persons he had ever met.

"People won't work for you long if you terrorize them all the time," Captain Gibson told Peter. "I can kill any one of my crew with my bare hands, but I never resort to violence with them- don't need to. The crew has my respect and I respect them." Gibson directed them back up on deck. "Have you ever been to England, Mr. Stewart?"

"No sir, but I'm more than ready to make the trip."

"It's quite a trip. I know you sailed up from Brunswick, but have you ever been on a boat for more than a day?"

Peter held back a laugh.

"Yes sir I have. I sailed for a couple of weeks straight one time a few years ago."

"If I may so bold to interrupt," Brown interjected politely. "Mr. Stewart is a fisherman."

"Oh, good. I might let you help the crew out."

The captain had a crew member show Peter and Mr. Brown to their quarters so they could store their belongings.

Later, Peter and Brown went up on deck to observe the activity. The Confidence had been loaded the previous evening and the crew was readying the sails. Captain Gibson was overseeing everything. He was quite a contrast to Captain Chester. Gibson hardly even said a word to his crew. Peter realized that Gibson's men were so well trained that they did not have to be told what to do.

Captain Gibson noticed Peter standing near the cabin doorway. "Mr. Stewart?" Gibson called. "I'd like to have a word with you."

Peter walked over to where Captain Gibson was standing.

"Yes sir? Looks like we'll have fine weather."

"Mr. Stewart, you're not an employee of Carey Exporters and it has come to my understanding that you have not paid any passage."

"That's true, but Mr. Brown said I could work unloading and loading cargo. I'll help out in any way you ask."

"There's been a change of plans. The company already has enough labor to load the cargo. We need someone to assist our navigator. You do know about navigation?"

This was Peter's specialty next to fishing. He did not get many opportunities for true navigation back home since he found Island Unknown.

"Yes sir. I *do* know something about navigating."

"Good, you'll be working with Mr. Braganza."

Captain Gibson had a crewman take Peter to meet the ship's navigator. Braganza was an odd sort of a man. He looked different from the other crewmen.

"Are you Peter?" Braganza asked when Peter entered the small cabin.

"Yes sir. Captain Gibson told me to help you."

"Yes. I just need someone to take over my duties when I'm asleep. Our assistant navigator has come down with fever and will stay here in Savannah." Braganza smiled. "There's really nothing hard about it. I only sleep about five hours a day."

"I've never heard an accent like yours. Where do you come from?" Peter questioned.

"I come from Portugal. I live in Liverpool when we are not out to sea." Braganza pointed to the map he had spread out on the table. "Here is where we are at. We will be sailing for the Azore Islands where we will resupply the ship." Braganza smiled. "I have family there."

Peter learned some new things about navigation from his discussions with Braganza. His family were well known as the company's top navigators. Braganza's older brother was a navigator on the Oriental route.

Chapter 4   The Azores

Peter was glad to again see the beautiful cobalt blue of the deep waters far offshore. He had been asleep as they sailed through the Gulf Stream. He enjoyed being able to watch such a large crew at work. He imagined what it would be like to captain a fishing boat so large.

On the fifth day at sea the ship encountered a terrible storm. Peter never fished in stormy weather back home. In fact, he had not sailed in such weather since the fierce storm he battled on the way to Island Unknown. The storm made him think about that time in his life. He wished that Grandpa was still alive to make the trip to England with him.

Each day Peter got to know more about The Confidence's navigator, Braganza. He had lived in several Portuguese colonies. Like Captain Chester, Braganza wanted to sail all over the world and perhaps discover a new land. Braganza knew of Captain Chester and hoped to be his navigator someday when he was promoted to international sea captain. Peter also got to know the crew better. Some of the crew were barely men. He was amazed at how knowledgeable and mature they were.

Since there were no other passengers, Peter spent a lot of his free time with Brown. Peter liked to listen to Brown talk about his boyhood in England. He learned many things about him that he did not know. Brown's father had wanted him to become a gentleman so he sent him to an expensive boarding school. This explained his genteel manner. Brown was a school teacher for a few years and then became a valet for an earl.

"You know, ol' Andrew thought you were some kind of nobility like an earl, or even a duke," Peter confided.

"Heavens no," Brown said while laughing. "I'm extremely flattered that he thought that of me, but I will assure him when we return that I'm quite the ordinary man. Besides, why would I move away from England if I were a duke?"

"So, were you ever married?" Peter asked him.

He sighed.

"I was. It was when I was a teacher. Rebecca was her name."

"Didn't work out or something?" Peter asked.

"To the contrary. We were quite happy. Rebecca passed away during the birth of our daughter. Our little angel died two days later."

Peter put his hand on Brown's shoulder. He nodded and wiped a tear from his eye.

"You know, Peter, some things you never get over."

<><><><>

As the days went on, Peter was becoming increasingly bored with the long sea voyage.

"I love to sail, but how do you stand these trips to and from England?" he asked Brown. "I'm tired of walking around this ship."

Brown nodded in agreement.

"I sympathize with you, Peter. I haven't made as many transatlantic voyages as my brother Charles, but I always wind up longing for land after a few days. We should be reaching the Azores soon." Brown patted Peter on the shoulder. "Try and remember that we could be sailing to China."

Much to Peter's amazement, their landfall in the Azores was within one hour of Braganza's prediction. Peter was thrilled to actually see land again. Brown joined Peter on deck. Brown was also glad to be able to walk upon solid ground. Peter was intrigued by the group of islands.

"Those sure are funny looking mountains," Peter stated as he referred to the cone-shaped hills."

"Those are dead volcanoes, Peter," Brown replied.

"I can't wait to tell Andrew and Mother I saw volcanoes. They won't believe me."

They sailed to a town called Ponta Delgada on the large island of Sao Miguel. The ports around the islands were incredibly deep. For the first time in his life Peter saw Spanish and Portuguese ships. Captain Gibson noticed Peter admiring the ships as they pulled into the harbor.

"I wouldn't be staring at that Spaniard ship, Mr. Stewart."

"Why is that? We're not at war with them, are we?"

"No, we're not fighting the Spaniards, but to them, this is a British ship. A lot of Spaniards don't get along too well with the British." Captain Gibson pointed at the Spanish ship. "Besides, that ship right there is The Seville. The captain on that ship hates me."

"He hates you? Why is that?"

"He thinks I killed his brother in a fight about eight years ago. I know who did it, but I wouldn't tell him who it was. So now he thinks that I was the killer."

Peter noticed The Seville's crew that was on deck began to eye them as they docked into port.

"If they only knew that I've got some of their queen's gold back home," Peter thought to himself.

It was Braganza's job to go ashore and arrange for supplies for the ship. Braganza had cousins who owned a market place in town. Captain Gibson sent for Braganza.

"I normally go ashore with Mr. Braganza, but not with those Spaniards sitting there. We seem to be the only friendly ship around, and we don't need any trouble."

Captain Gibson allowed Peter and Mr. Brown to accompany Braganza. Braganza's cousin had already closed his business so they went to his house.

"We'll be staying the night here," Braganza said. "My cousin's wife is very beautiful. When I first saw her I could not stop watching her. My cousin saw this and introduced me to his wife's younger sister. I married her four years ago."

Brown and Peter laughed. Braganza knocked on his cousin's front door.

"I must apologize, but from now on I must speak Portuguese."

Brown and Peter were both taken aback by the woman who answered the door. She was clearly the most beautiful woman Peter had ever seen. She quickly hugged Braganza and called to her husband. Braganza's cousin was one of the friendliest and hospitable persons Peter had ever run across. Even though he spoke no English; he treated both Brown and Peter like they were family. Braganza's cousin had three children who were fascinated with Peter because he came from America. They had many questions for Peter about himself and his life in America. Brown knew a few phrases of Portuguese and Braganza helped translate. They all stayed up rather late visiting and playing games with the children.

Braganza awakened Peter and Brown before sunrise the next day. Braganza and his cousin went to the market place to gather enough food and water to resupply the ship. Meanwhile, Peter and Brown were treated to an unusual breakfast. Peter had never eaten most of the fruit that was given to him. Brown and Peter thanked the beautiful lady for the meal and said goodbye to the children. They headed towards the docks where the crew was loading the supplies from the Braganzas.

Captain Gibson was having a discussion with Braganza and a stranger. Peter learned the captain of The Seville had ordered Gibson to leave by sunset after learning that The Confidence would be sailing at mid morning anyway. Peter was sorry that they were leaving so soon. He enjoyed being with Braganza's family. He especially enjoyed being on land for a change.

The captain of The Seville seemed to be enjoying himself as he saw The Confidence weigh anchor and begin to head out of the harbor. He and Captain Gibson gave one another hard looks, but neither said anything as The Confidence passed by The Seville.

"We won't be alone on our way back through here," Captain Gibson said as he continued staring at the Spanish ship. "Next time we'll be staying in here Porta Delgado for as long as we want."

Chapter 5   England and the Search for the Mystery

Peter did not feel as restless as he was before they landed at the Azores. He knew that England, and a possible answer to his curiosity, might be there waiting for him.

The Confidence encountered another storm the day after leaving Sao Miguel. They also passed a Dutch ship that was heading south to the Antilles.

As they neared England, the air became much cooler. It was much different than the balmy weather of Georgia. Peter spent a great deal of time looking at Braganza's maps. It was very exciting for him to realize how close he was to Europe. He wished that the ship had been sailing close enough to shore so he could actually see the western coast of Portugal, or the northern coasts of Spain and France.

The Confidence sailed into Liverpool's harbor while he and Brown were asleep so Peter was disappointed not to experience the entry. As soon as Peter awakened, he realized that the ship was no longer in motion.

"Wake up Brown; we've stopped. We must be *here*."

Peter and Brown got dressed and went on deck. Activity on the docks was just starting to pick up. There were several ships being loaded, or unloaded, by dozens of dockhands. The crew of The Confidence was already busy unloading the load of tobacco.

"Well sir, how do you like my home city?" Brown asked Peter.

"I like it a great deal," Peter said. "He looked out across the buildings and houses of the city. "And you say London is bigger than this?"

Brown laughed.

"Oh, many times bigger, Peter. Perhaps someday you will see it."

Peter and Brown went to find Captain Gibson. Brown wanted to see if he would have breakfast with them in the city, but he declined.

Peter quickly went below deck to get their bags. Then they walked onto the dock.

"Where are we going to sleep, and how long are we going to stay here?"

We shall be staying with my sister and her family for two or three days."

Brown paid a carriage driver to take them to his sister's house. It was the first time Peter had ever ridden in a paid carriage. All the streets they rode on were paved in brick. He was amazed at all of the two story houses and buildings. The hotel was the only two story building back home.

Brown's sister, Vivian, lived in a good sized two story house on a tree lined street. She closely resembled Brown and was just as genteel in manner. Peter was surprised that Brown's sister had a housekeeper.

"You mean they don't have to do any cooking or cleaning? Your sister's family actually *pays* someone to do that for them?" Peter shook his head. "My boss Mr. Milton is one of the richest men in town and he doesn't even have a housekeeper."

After Brown and Peter visited with Vivian's family and set their belongings in a guest bedroom, they walked over to a cafe to have breakfast. It was one of the fanciest breakfasts that Peter had ever eaten.

"I suppose I should be getting over to the warehouse," Brown said. He neatly folded the fine linen napkin. "The warehouse manager will want to talk to me now that he knows I'm here." Brown handed the waitress some coins for their meal. "I'm sure the manager has a few Americans working for him. We'll have to ask him about your mysterious American and that watch business."

Peter and Mr. Brown paid for a ride over to the warehouse. The building was enormous. There were probably three hundred crates of furniture and other items. Some crates were marked *China, France, Germany*, and a few said *Italy*. Peter and Brown found the warehouse manager at the back of the warehouse. He seemed especially happy to see Brown.

"There's the man I was looking for," the manager said as he shook Brown's hand. "How's that franchise of yours, Mr. Brown?"

"It's doing quite well. I have no competition where I am at." Brown turned to Peter. "This is Peter Stewart. I have my warehouse on his property. He's assisting me with my shipment. Peter, this is Paul Bronson; he's in charge of this impressive operation you see before you."

Brown and Bronson worked together in getting the shipment in order. After they had designated which crates were to go back with Brown, they all had tea in Bronson's tiny office.

"Mr. Bronson? When my oldest brother was here last he met an American man employed here who gave him a small company crate to take back to Georgia for Mr. Stewart here. How many Americans do you have employed at present?"

"I've three, but one of them just started last week," Bronson said. "What's this all about?"

"This American man had dark hair." Peter paused. "It was a small crate that had a watch my father was wearing when he died at sea."

Bronson nodded rapidly.

"I think I know the man. Just a moment and I'll summon him." Bronson paused for a moment at the doorway. "Mr. Brown, you said this young man's name was Stewart?"

"Yes," Peter and Brown both answered together.

"Now isn't that curious. This American man I've got working for me has the same last name- *Stewart*."

Peter's heart started to race as soon as he heard Bronson say the name *Stewart*. He looked at Brown. Even he was now at the edge of his seat with anticipation.

A few minutes later Bronson came back with a dark haired man. Peter and Brown looked at each other and smirked. The man was barely over five feet tall. Brown took Bronson aside.

"My brother says the man was tall."

Bronson sent the man away.

"Nobody around here like. The only person I know working for the company that looks like that is a part owner. I *think* he's an American. He only talked to me once and he definitely didn't have the full British accent. He always sends an assistant to do business. It couldn't have been him though. He wouldn't come down here to talk to your brother Charles."

Peter and Brown left the warehouse and returned to Brown's sister's house. Peter sat down on one of the fine chairs in the parlor. He had been hoping to get answers about his father's watch and now he was full of more questions.

Later, after lunch, Brown showed him the city and the country side. This helped Peter temporarily forget his disappointment. He hardly said a word during the tour as he and Brown rode in his brother-in-law's carriage.

"I see your mind is still working on that misfortune of not finding the American," Brown said. He steered the carriage to the side of the road and stopped for a moment.

"I should have known that I couldn't find him. I don't even think he wants to be found."

"That exact thought has crossed my mind, Peter." Brown gave a sly smile. "He wishes to remain anonymous. We shan't give up yet. To get your mind off the disappointment we shall do something special this evening."

"*Special?*" Peter asked.

"Yes. After dinner we shall visit my gentleman's club and then we can go to my favorite pub." Brown directed the carriage horse back into the road and they were off again.

"A pub? Is it like the Lighthouse Tavern?"

"Actually, the Bull's Head Pub is like the Lighthouse Tavern in some ways."

"I would have never guessed that *you* would go to a pub."

Brown stopped the horses in front of his brother-in-law's carriage house. He put his hand on Peter's shoulder.

"How would you like a new suit, Peter?"

"I wouldn't mind one since the one I got is too small, but Mother just hadn't the time to make me a new one. Besides, all I've got is a little American money on me."

"Never mind the money. I can pay for the suit." Brown looked down at Peter's feet. "I see you will be needing a new pair of shoes as well."

Brown and Peter climbed back into the carriage and headed over to a clothing store not far from the harbor. Brown picked out a dark suit for Peter and a pair of black shoes.

Peter enjoyed being in Liverpool. He could hardly believe that he was so far from home. He wondered what was happening with his mother and how his cousin Andrew was doing. This was definitely the longest time that Peter had been away from home.

Later, Peter, Brown, and Vivian's family sat down to dinner. They were joined by Brown's nephew, his wife and baby.

Right after dinner Brown and Peter dressed and rode over to the gentleman's club that Brown belonged to. Andrew had told Peter about the gentleman's club that the plantation owners had in back in Savannah. He wondered if this one was similar.

"Please try not to be intimidated by this place, or the people inside," Brown advised Peter. "These people are not the stuffy, arrogant type you might be expecting to encounter."

The building where the club was located was much smaller than Peter thought it would be.

"My club was formed in this very building over two hundred years ago. My great-great, great grandfather was the first in the family to join," Brown said proudly.

Most all of the twenty members were inside the parlor. They were pleasantly surprised to see Brown. The members did not treat Peter like he was an outsider. In fact, they were interested in his knowledge of the sea and his experience with finding Spanish treasure. Peter and Brown stayed for over two hours and then headed over to the Bull's Head Pub.

"Let's take off our ties so we'll look much more casual, eh Peter?"

"You won't tell my mother that I was in a pub will you?"

"Of course not. I wouldn't like it if she knew that I was in a pub either."

The surroundings of the pub were different than the Lighthouse Tavern. There were many different bottles of liquor on display. All in all, it was much more livelier.

Peter had been expecting to meet someone that resented him for being an American, but this was not the case. He found out quickly that American merchantmen frequently visited the Bull's Head. Peter had conversations with several of Brown's friends. He particularly enjoyed talking with an Irishman that was the same age as him.

A little later, several of The Confidence's crew members entered the pub. They said hello to Brown and Peter and then sat down at another table. Not long after that Captain Gibson came in with Braganza and two strangers.

"Who's that with Captain Gibson?" Peter asked Brown.

Brown looked at them closely.

I believe one of them is a ship captain. The other gentleman works for the company. In fact, Mr. Bronson, the warehouse manager you met, answers to *him*. He's the general manager's new assistant. Mr. Reece is his name."

Peter looked over at Braganza hoping to subtly attract his attention, but he was engaged in conversation with the ship captains.

"Perhaps we could ask the gentleman if he knows about that watch that was sent to you," Brown suggested. "Do you have it in your possession"?

"Yes. I have the watch with me. I've been keeping it with me ever since we talked to Mr. Bronson. I wanted to be ready just in case we found somebody who would remember the watch."

After a few minutes, Peter and Brown walked over to Captain Gibson's table.

"Good evening, Mr. Brown, Mr. Stewart," Captain Gibson said cordially. "Peter, I want you to meet Captain Jackson and, Brown, I'm sure you know Mr. Reece here."

Brown shook Mr. Reece's hand. "That's quite right. In fact, it was Mr. Reece who suggested I open a franchise store in Brunswick." Brown gave Peter a quick look. "I had thought Connecticut might be a more profitable locality, but Mr. Reece convinced me to choose Brunswick. How are you Mr. Reece?"

"I'm quite fine," Mr. Reece said. "How do you like Georgia? I see by the records that our store has gotten off to a jolly good start."

"Yes it has done well thus far. It is expensive for the townspeople, but they enjoy the merchandise." Brown and Peter sat down at the table. "I certainly thank you for urging me to open the business in Brunswick. I do appreciate the close proximity to my brother in Savannah."

"Splendid, Brown. You're quite welcome. Tell me, have you become well acquainted with the people there?"

"Why yes I have. As a matter of fact Mr. Stewart here who accompanied me across the Atlantic is from Brunswick." Brown put his hand on Peter's shoulder. "I'd like to introduce you to the top fisherman in town, Peter Stewart."

For a second Mr. Reece became nervous. He regained his composure and extended his hand toward Peter.

"Mr. Reece, I understand you are an assistant to the general manager of the company?" Peter asked.

"Well sir, I also work for the owner. Mrs. Carey still owns half the company. When Mr. Carey passed away he gave half the business to his assistant, Mr. Monroe. He is the general manager, but I do handle many of the administrative tasks for Mr. Monroe."

"Perhaps you could help us Mr. Reece?" Brown added. "Mr. Stewart was sent a small crate through my brother Charles when he was last here. My brother said a tall, American man with dark hair asked him to deliver it to Peter Stewart in Brunswick."

Peter reached into his pocket and put the watch on the table.

"This watch was in the crate. Could you look at it? You might remember it."

Again, Reece became nervous. He quickly handed the watch back to Peter.

"There's an inscription on it. See, it says..."

Mr. Reece interrupted Peter.

"Please sir, take this matter up with Mr. Bronson our warehouse manager. I have no knowledge of the contents of every crate that is shipped by the company. We have hundreds of crates leaving our warehouse every month."

Mr. Reece excused himself and quickly left the pub.

"Well, he sure became stuffy when you showed him that watch," Captain Gibson remarked.

Peter was about to say something, but Brown stopped him.

"Let me buy each of you fine gentlemen a drink."

Brown and Peter stayed at the pub and talked with the captains and Braganza for about an hour before heading back to Vivian's house.

Peter was quiet for most of the ride home and refused to engage in small talk with Brown. He finally had enough.

"How come you didn't want to talk about the way Mr. Reece acted when I showed him the watch?" Peter asked.

"I let the matter go because I knew that Mr. Reece was lying," Brown answered sternly.

"Lying? You think that Mr. Reece sent me the watch?"

"No. It's a very curious situation though. Reece probably knows who sent you the watch." Brown rested his hand on Peter's shoulder for a second. "Peter, we have become good friends since I arrived in Georgia. Andrew and your mother have been very kind and hospitable to me. In some ways I feel like I am a part of your family."

"Well, I kind of think of you as sort of an uncle," Peter confessed. "You know my grandpa's first name was Richard just like yours."

Brown smiled briefly.

"I must admit that I was skeptical about that being your father's watch. I thought that bringing you here would help erase your hope of finding the whereabouts of your father. Until tonight I was sure that your father had perished at sea, but now I wonder if perhaps he survived a shipwreck or whatever calamity fell upon him."

Peter was speechless. He never told Brown that he thought his father might still be alive.

"I am of the opinion he at least survived for a time," Brown continued. "Your father may not be alive now, but whoever sent his watch to you knows what happened to him." Brown thought for a moment. "Mr. Monroe. He is the new part owner of the company. I have never met the man personally, but have only heard about him through Mr. Reece or Mr. Bronson at the warehouse. We shall pay Mr. Monroe a visit tomorrow. He may be the one person who can help us get to the bottom of this unpleasant mystery."

Peter had a difficult time sleeping that night because he was so excited. Peter had always respected Brown's wisdom and high intelligence. For him to say that he believed his father had not died at sea gave Peter great hope. Until now, Peter was convinced that Brown was just humoring him by taking him to England.

The next morning Brown's brother-in-law, Paul, insisted on taking Peter and Brown to his place of work. Paul was a bookkeeper for several of the businesses in the city. Peter had to stay there for an agonizing two hours and listen to Paul discuss the detailed finances of the accounts he was responsible for before they could leave to find Mr. Monroe.

Brown found a driver and had him take them to the warehouse so that Mr. Bronson could give them directions Mr. Monroe's house. Mr. Monroe lived about a half a mile from the center of Liverpool. He had a fairly large home, but it was by no means as spectacular as the plantation mansions Peter had seen near Savannah when he had visited Andrew's family.

Brown and Peter climbed out of the coach and walked up the small flight of stairs to the front door. Brown knocked loudly on the beautifully carved door.

"Please allow me to speak for you if I may."

Peter nodded in agreement.

"Do you have the watch?"

Peter felt his shirt pocket and nodded again. Just then a middle-aged man opened the door.

"Good morning, sir. I hope you are doing well this fine day," Brown said. "Is this residence of Mr. Monroe?"

The man nodded once.

"Splendid. I am Richard Brown and this is Mr. Peter Stewart. I am the owner of the franchise store in Brunswick, Georgia."

"*Brunswick?*" The man seemed to either not to know that the company had a store there, or had never heard of Georgia.

"Yes, Brunswick. In the United States. We need to discuss a business matter with Mr. Monroe."

"Well, Mr. Monroe is not here."

"What time do you expect him back?"

"Back?" The man seemed confused. "Well sirs, Mr. Monroe is in France." There was a long silence. "Mr. Monroe should be back in three or four days, perhaps even a week. He is on a buying excursion for the company. You gentlemen should talk with Mr. Bronson at the warehouse, or perhaps Mr. Reece. Mr. Monroe *never* handles any of the matters of employees or even franchise owners such as yourself."

Peter and Brown looked at each other and then walked back to the coach. Peter was extremely disappointed. He said nothing as the carriage driver took them back to Vivian's house.

"Every time we inquire about the watch someone refers us back to Mr. Bronson." Brown said trying to sympathize with Peter.

Peter sighed heavily.

"I don't know, but I almost feel like throwing the watch in the ocean."

"Now, you can't mean that Peter. That watch is a part of your father, *and* your grandfather."

"That's right. I was happy until I got this watch. I thought I had finally buried the memory of my father. This whole trip has been a waste of time. We're leaving tomorrow and I still don't know anything about the person who sent the watch."

Brown said nothing. He realized that words were meaningless in this situation. Back at Vivian's house, Brown went inside the parlor to spend time with his sister. Peter started walking around Liverpool. He suddenly had memories of his father that he had not had in years. Peter took out the watch and read the inscription that he had read a hundred times already. He gripped the watch tightly in his hand. Peter almost smashed the watch against a brick building, but something inside himself stopped him at the last second. He eventually wandered over to the docks. Some men from the warehouse were loading crates onto The Confidence. Peter sat down and watched them. Braganza was on board with a woman and a toddler and saw Peter sitting there. He decided to go over and talk to him.

"Is this your wife and little daughter?" Peter asked.

Braganza introduced them.

"I was showing them the ship I spend most of my life on. I may have to sneak them aboard tomorrow."

"Well I won't say a word to Captain Gibson," Peter joked. "If you bring them down to Brunswick they can stay with my family as long as you want."

"Did you find what you were looking for here in Liverpool?" Braganza asked.

Peter thought for a moment.

"Yes and no. I found out that there really never *was* anything to find out."

Braganza nodded and smiled.

"I'm sorry that you had to travel such a great distance to find out that what you are looking for is in Georgia. That is your home and it is your life."

Chapter 6   Mr. Monroe

Peter started walking back to Vivian's house. It was late afternoon and he began to accept the fact that he was not going to get answers about his father. Since he had not eaten since that morning he was starving. Brown did not ask where he had been and stayed off the subject of the watch. Brown's niece and her husband were there for dinner. Peter now realized that Brown had not had much time to spend with his family because he had been helping him find out who sent the watch. Peter felt guilty for being selfish. He had hardly said anything to Vivian or her husband during his stay. In fact, Peter had not even taken the time to look around the house. It was a beautiful home with many unusual items that Brown had gotten from far away places.

Peter started socializing with Brown's niece and her husband. She had her beautiful baby in her arms. They all had a delicious meal followed by an interesting conversation. At about half past seven there was a knock on the door. Someone wanted to talk with Brown. Peter ignored the man at the door because he figured it was someone discussing his shipment. After a moment Brown became very excited and asked Peter to come to the door.

"This man works for Mr. Monroe. He says that Monroe has just arrived and will speak to you about the watch!"

Peter had completely wiped those thoughts out of his mind. Now Peter could feel the weight of the watch in his pocket. He had not noticed it since the afternoon.

"Well come now Peter. Let's go speak with Mr. Monroe." Brown said. He patted Peter on the back rapidly and then quickly put his jacket on.

The man at the door interrupted.

"I am terribly sorry sir, but Mr. Monroe said only Mr. Stewart was to come."

Peter and Brown looked at one another. Peter could see that he was disappointed.

"Oh well, it's quite understandable. The watch *does* belong to Mr. Stewart's father."

Peter followed the man to a coach that was waiting out front. Peter decided to take advantage of the opportunity to ask the man about Mr. Monroe.

"I understand Mr. Monroe owns half the company?"

"That's right, mista. Mr. Monroe took over 'alf of it when old Mr. Carey passed on, he did."

"Mr. Monroe is an *American?*"

"I can't rightly say. He's got a bit of an accent, but not like most in Liverpool. I just work for the man. I never ask no questions. He says drive here; drive there and I do it. Monroe's a quiet man who keeps to 'imself. He's got no wife nor kids; I know that much, I do. I once 'eard 'im speak French and Portuguese, but I 'ave no idea where Monroe come from, sir. Like I said, I do me job and don't ask questions. I mostly takes me orders from the butler, Mr. Jackson."

Peter was driven up to the front walk of Monroe's house and let out.

"Just give a knock on the door," the driver told Peter. "Mr. Jackson will answer. I'll take ya' back when Mr. Jackson tells me to, sir."

Peter's heart began pounding. It had been a long time since he felt this nervous. He knocked softly on the door. There was a long silence before he heard footsteps approaching. The door opened slowly. It was the same man who had answered the door earlier for him and Brown.

"Good evening, Mr. Stewart. Mr. Monroe arrived a little over an hour ago. He is eager to speak with you."

The butler led Peter to a study just before the staircase to the second floor.

"Mr. Monroe shall be here shortly," the butler said. He pointed to a chair in front of an enormous desk. "Please sit *here*."

Peter waited until the butler left and began looking at everything in the study. He gazed at the guns and swords attached to the wall above the fireplace. The rest of the study walls were covered with fine paintings and every shelf had beautiful vases and statues on them. Nothing in Brown's store compared to what Peter saw in that study. He had never seen so many books in his life. Mr. Monroe was obviously a well educated man. Peter looked down at the rug underneath him. It had an unusual pattern. He wondered if it was from China.

Peter heard footsteps approaching so he moved away from the bookshelves and sat down in the chair in front of the huge desk. Peter had to turn in his seat to see who it was coming down the hall. Just then, a tall bearded man entered the room. He was smiling.

"Peter Stewart? You *are* the Peter Stewart from Brunswick, Georgia?"

"Yes sir," Peter answered. He was cautious in his answer because the man acted like he knew of him.

Mr. Monroe stood next to a chair by the fireplace.

"Please, sit in this chair next to me. Jackson always puts the guests in front of that big desk so they'll have to look up at the *powerful* Mr. Monroe."

He waited for Peter to bring his chair. Mr. Monroe extended his hand. He was slightly taller than Peter. His accent was hard to place. It was a blend of English, American and something else.

"So you're Mr. Monroe?"

The man laughed and then shrugged his shoulders. He gestured for Peter to take his seat and the two sat down at the same time.

"You could say that." Again, he had a grin as he stared at Peter. "So you're *Peter William Stewart*, huh? Your grandpa is *Richard William Stewart*?"

"Yes sir that is our given names. My grandfather died a few years ago."

Monroe's smile quickly left his face. He looked down at his shoes and was silent for a moment.

"Your mother, Margaret; is she well?" Mr. Monroe asked hesitantly.

"She's doing well, sir."

"Good. Good. How about yourself? What kind of work do you do?"

"My cousin and I are fishermen. I have my own boat that my grandfather built for me."

Again, Monroe beamed at Peter.

"A *fisherman* are you? Oh, I am happy for you. I know that boat you have is a strong one."

There was a long silence. Peter could not stand being uncomfortable any longer. He reached into his shirt pocket and removed the watch.

"Mr. Monroe, this watch was sent to me by an American who works your company. Now before you ask me to talk to Mr. Bronson just know that I already have. He said there is no American working for him that matches the man's description."

Monroe took the watch from Peter's hand. He looked at it and smiled before handing it back to Peter. Monroe then stood up and walked over to the bookshelves.

"*I* sent the watch."

Peter figured it was him because he matched the description that Brown's brother had given.

"Excuse me sir, but I don't understand all this. I know that you are an important man and all, but I don't understand how you came across my father's watch. Did you find it, or buy it from someone? You know all about my family, but I have to apologize and tell you that I don't know you, sir."

Monroe still had his back towards Peter.

"No, I did not *find* it." He sighed heavily. "It's mine. That's *my* watch."

"What?!" Peter exclaimed. "*No.*"

Monroe turned to face Peter.

"I was afraid you wouldn't know who I was. You don't recognize me, Peter?"

Peter shook his head.

"I suppose it's been too long. I'm John Stewart- *your father.*"

Peter looked away. He felt like he was in a nightmare.

"No sir. My father would have gone back home as soon as he could, but he was shipwrecked or killed by pirates."

Monroe stepped towards Peter and looked him in the eye.

"No I wasn't. I wasn't lost at sea." He again sat down in the chair next to Peter. He could tell by Peter's body movements that he was uncomfortable so he spoke calmly.

"What did your mother tell you about me being lost at sea?"

Peter sighed heavily.

She told me that my *father* was killed in a storm while out fishing. My Grandpa told me the true story just before he died."

"Well, then you know about me trying to find the island?"

Peter shrugged his shoulders.

"Your mother and I had strong disagreements over me looking for that treasure. I couldn't make her understand that I just *had* to go. I didn't have time because the man who told me how to get to the island was on his deathbed. I wanted to put some of that gold into his hands so he could die knowing that somebody found it."

Peter did not say anything, but inside, he remembered his mother's opposition to his own search for the treasure.

"I don't know why, but your mother grew to hate the fact that I was a fisherman. She wanted us to move to Savannah near her parents and start a farm." Monroe looked over at Peter. He was attentive and seemed less uncomfortable so he went on. "It didn't take long for folks in town to know that I was planning to go find the treasure. I would've looked like a fool if I didn't go. People were either urging me to go find the island, or saying I was not man enough to try it. There was this one lowlife of a man. We called him *Leech*. I can't remember his last name. Oh, he was the worst. Every day he would call me yellow or a boy. I really hated that man."

"You mean Mr. Myers? He's still in town," Peter interrupted.

"He's still alive?" Monroe shook his head. "I thought he would have drunk himself to death. I guess he's still running everyone down; that old coot."

"He's not a coot anymore. He's been *saved*."

Monroe laughed loudly.

"God almighty. I guess if the Lord can create the world in six days he can save a wretch like Leech."

Peter actually laughed a little with Mr. Monroe.

"Every day I think about the mistake I made in trying to find that island. I must have sailed right past it while I was sleeping. I was in such a rush that I didn't think things through. My father kept telling I wasn't doing it right. I didn't keep track of my locations while I was asleep. I did turn around and I sailed the course back west and tried to stay awake, but I was so exhausted from a lack of sleep. That's when I made the biggest mistake of my life. How could I face everyone back home? I knew your mother would never want me to try and find the island a second time. I would regret not finding it or not going back just like Robert Jenkins. Everyone would hate me. My own son would grow up thinking his father was a failure. I figured it would be better if everyone thought I died. So, I turned around and headed east again only this time I didn't turn back. I just kept sailing east. Of course, I couldn't find the island. You've got to understand what it's like out there alone on the ocean. A person can go crazy. I wasn't thinking straight. After a few days I changed my plan. I would to go to Europe, become wealthy, and then return a hero."

Peter was highly interested in Monroe's story. He was still a bit skeptical, but there was something that made him genuine.

"What happened after that?" Peter asked. "Didn't you run out of food and especially water?"

"Food? Oh, I had plenty of fish to catch. I ran out of water two days before I reached Portugal. I had hoped to catch some rainwater, but it never rained. I finally landed at Cadiz, Portugal. I hated to do it, but I sold my boat and went to work as a deck hand on a Portuguese merchant ship. I worked for a couple of years or so on a route to England. During this time I made friends with some people here in Liverpool. They asked me what my name was and before I knew it I was telling them I was from Florida Territory and my name was John Monroe. Anyway, one of those people was Mr. Carey. Even back then Mr. Carey was an old man." Monroe smiled for a moment. "He reminded me a great deal of my grandfather. You never met him, but he was a lot like your grandfather. Mr. Carey had that same way of thinking as my grandpa and yours. Mr. Carey liked me a lot. I guess you could say I was like a son to him. I went to work for Mr. Carey and after a few years he hired me as manager of his business. The job Mr. Reece has now. I owe *everything* to Mr. Carey. He was the man who educated me. You know, I could hardly read my own name before I met him and now I can read books on medicine, philosophy, and poetry. I confided to Mr. and Mrs. Carey about my real identity. They were disappointed, but sympathetic. A couple of years before Mr. Carey died he and Mrs. Carey decided that upon his death they would give half ownership of the business to me."

"You became a rich man *then*. Why didn't you return home like you said?"

Monroe got up and walked over to the bookshelves again.

"I tried to. Do you know I even sailed to Boston and Philadelphia several years ago? I was too scared to go to Georgia. I thought I would write a letter first, but as the years went by I even lost the courage to write. By then I thought that you and your mother figured I was dead. I imagined your mother had gotten married again. I guess that's the case? She remarried?"

Peter was feeling even more empty of emotions now.

"No, she never got married again. So why bother trying to get to know me now? Why send the watch now?"

"I had hoped to visit you some day. I wanted to gradually let you know I was still alive. I sent the watch to build up my courage. I had Mr. Reece strongly urge Mr. Brown to set up the franchise in Brunswick."

"So Brown really had no idea what was going on?" Peter asked.

"Oh, no. *No sir.* I don't think I've even met the man."

"How about his brother, Charles? Did he know all about this?"

"*I* gave him the watch myself. I paid him extra for his troubles. He didn't ask any questions." He sat down again. "I *had* to see you. I think about you and your mother every day. I guess I finally grew up and now I want to pay for the biggest mistake of my life."

Peter shook his head and smiled.

"I grew up hearing nothing but great things about my father. I must admit that it did seem strange for an experienced sailor to get lost at sea. I figured it was one of those storms or pirates. Why would such a *great* man turn his back on his family just because some townsfolk would make fun of him? I'm still young, but I know that family is everything. I'd die without my family."

"That's the *point*, Peter. I wasn't the perfect man I'm sure your grandfather told you about. I wasn't a man inside and I was a coward for not acting like a man."

Peter laughed.

"I remember this huge man with a beard, but I can't tell if you're the same person or not. I was too young. You look too thin and pale to be him. All I remember is my father made toy boats for me."

"*That's right.* You floated them in the horse trough," he interrupted.

Peter did not say anything, but the man was right.

"If you are my father I always thought that you were the one who had the strong spirit."

Monroe's eyes began to water.

"No, it's *you* who's a man. I sure am proud of the man you have become."

Peter thought about telling him about his discovery of Island Unknown, but he decided against it.

Monroe got up and went over to his desk. He took out a sealed letter.

"This letter is for your mother. I see you may not believe I am your father, but after your mother reads this you'll be convinced." He handed Peter the letter. "There's things in here that only she and I know."

Peter reached into his pocket and took out the watch.

"Do you want this back?"

Monroe looked at the watch and smiled.

"No, it's yours now. That old watch has been through a lot. I was almost killed three times by people who wanted it. That watch was the only thing I had left from Georgia. It's important to me and I want you to have it." He looked at the clock on the wall and then motioned for Peter to follow him. "I wish you could stay longer, but I know your ship leaves in the morning. When Mr. Reece told me that you had come to Liverpool with Mr. Brown I was so excited that I decided to just go ahead and meet you." He continued walking Peter out the front door and to the coach. "If after speaking with your mother you decide you want to meet with me again just write me through the company. I tell you I'll be on a ship to Georgia as soon as I get your letter. The company just had a steamship built and they say it can cross the Atlantic three times as fast as our clipper ships."

"I'll keep that in mind."

Mr. Monroe extended his hand and the two shook.

"I've been praying that you and your mother will let me back in. You know, I've been faithful to your mother all these years."

Peter climbed into the coach and stared straight ahead.

The driver cracked his whip and the carriage scurried down the drive.

"Mr. Monroe must fancy you, sir," the driver said.

Peter was in a daze and hardly heard him.

"What's that?"

"I said Mr. Monroe must think right 'ighly of you because I've never seen 'im so 'appy around anyone, except the widow Carey."

It was late and very dark when Peter got back to Vivian's house. He quietly walked up the steps to the door and crept inside.

"Hello Peter," a voice whispered in the dark.

"Brown? What are you doing sitting there in the dark?"

"I was curious to know what Mr. Monroe had to say."

Peter felt around for a chair and sat down.

"Mr. Monroe said *he* was the one who sent me the watch." Peter whispered. "He also said that the watch was his."

"*Good Lord*, man," Brown said out loud. He quickly gained his composure and began to whisper again. "So it was *him* who sent it? Do you believe this man to be your father?"

"I don't know. It's been so long that I can't tell you one way or the other. He did know things, but... oh, *wait*." Peter reached into his pocket. "He gave me this letter to take to my mother. He said there's things in this letter that will prove he's my father."

"We must then wait until your mother can confirm this man's claim. You will show it to her?"

Peter sighed heavily.

"I think I should let her read it just to clear all this up. I hate the fact that this is going to bring up a lot of pain to my mother. She's already been through so much. I'll have a long sea voyage to think of a way to tell her."

"That's quite right, and please know I'll help you in any way I can."

Peter and Brown started walking to the guest room. Brown held the door open for Peter and stopped him when he entered the room.

"Peter, I can tell you right now if this Mr. Monroe is lying he will not escape the punishment he deserves. I will *personally* have the authorities remove him as head of the company. I need to schedule a meeting with Mrs. Carey before our ship leaves. She needs to know about what this imposter is doing."

"Don't bother. The Careys knew everything even before they gave him half the company."

Peter had a difficult time sleeping. The events of the evening had him confused and wondering. Over and over he tried to compare his recollection of what his father looked like to Mr. Monroe. He also considered what his future actions regarding Mr. Monroe would be.

"If he is my father I don't know if I could forgive him for what he did to Mother, Grandpa, and to me," Peter thought to himself. "If he's lying he'll have to explain himself to *me* and not to Brown or his authorities. But why would anyone but him be doing this to me?"

Peter had been asleep about an hour when Brown awakened.

"We mustn't be late, Peter. Captain Gibson will be angry if we're not on his ship in time."

Vivian was already making breakfast for them when Peter came downstairs. After breakfast, Peter and Brown gathered their things into the coach. Brown's brother-in-law then drove them to the docks.

The crew was loading the last of the food supplies on board. Peter took the bags on board while Brown said goodbye to his sister and her husband. Peter said hello to Captain Gibson and Braganza. The Confidence had a different crew of deckhands so the others could have some time off. Peter met the new crew members. The sun was just starting to lighten the sky. Brown and Peter stood on the dock side of The Confidence and watched a couple of crewmen pull away the gang plank from the dock.

"I always feel a bit sad leaving this town and my family." Brown turned to Peter and smiled. "But, I do have a new home now and new friends."

Peter nodded and smiled. He and Brown waved goodbye to Vivian. Captain Gibson ordered for the anchors to be pulled in. Just then, another coach drove up next to Vivian's. Peter instantly recognized the coach driver. A man stepped out of the coach.

"It's *him*, Brown. That's Mr. Monroe, or the man who might be my father.

Brown took a long look at the man as they slowly drifted away from the dock.

"I'm quite sure that I've never met the man." Brown took a quick look at Peter and then continued looking at Mr. Monroe. "There is a strong similarity in appearance between you both."

"Are you saying that I look like Mr. Monroe?"

"Yes Peter, but again, that could be coincidence."

Peter looked over Liverpool one more time.

"Goodbye Liverpool. I might return some day."

Mr. Monroe waved to Peter. Peter hesitated and then returned his wave.

Chapter 7   Back Across the Atlantic

The Confidence made a quick stop in Dublin to pick up a small shipment for Brown's brother in Savannah. Like Liverpool, Dublin was an interesting city to Peter. He wanted to wander around the city a bit, but they were only there for an hour.

Peter decided to get even more involved with this crew after they left Dublin. He felt guilty about not helping the other crew on the way to England. He still spent time navigating with Braganza. He was impressed with how many calculations the navigator had to make. Peter often relieved the crew members so they could get some extra sleep. Every crew member had several stories about their experiences on the sea. Three of the crew members confided to Peter that they had been pirates at sea and thieves on land.

It was during the voyage back across the Atlantic that Peter got to know one of the crew members in particular. The man's name was John. Since there were two other men on board named John they were named after where they were from. John had been born and raised in Africa so the crew called him African John. The other two deckhands were known as Irish John and Formby John. Back in Georgia African John would be a slave, but he was a free man in England and the company paid him regular sailor's wages. Peter had met and known many wise men, but none were wiser than John. He told Peter all about his life before he came to England. In the Windward Coast area of Africa, John had been an important warrior. His father was the leader of the village they lived in.

John had an effect on Peter. He was the most fascinating person Peter had ever met. John envied people like Brown. His dream was to move to America and live the rest of his life as a shopkeeper. John wanted to own a store in America and sell items for the Carey Company.

During the evenings Peter had conversations with Brown. He had not brought up the subject of Mr. Monroe until they were near the Azores.

"Tell me Peter; have you decided to give your mother the letter that Mr. Monroe gave you?"

"I'm going to give it to her. My mother's one strong lady. She knows how to deal with pain."

"This Monroe fellow; did he ask about your life?"

"Yes sir, he did. He asked me what trade I was in and how my mother was and all." Peter smiled and shook his head. "I asked him some questions too. I even asked him if *you* knew about Monroe sending the watch."

"Good Heavens, Peter," said an amazed Brown. "You thought that *I* was involved in this conspiracy?"

"No, not really. I had to be sure though. He did say that it was his idea to try and get you to open your store in Brunswick. Course Mr. Reece did all the talking for him."

"That he did. I was planning to open up in Connecticut until Mr. Reece spoke to me. The company offered to pay for my house and the building for the store if I moved to Brunswick. I trust you will not tell anyone in town about that."

"Mr. Brown, I haven't heard a word you've said," Peter said with a sly grin.

"Thank you, sir. Did Mr. Monroe know of your journey to Island Unknown and the treasure you discovered there?"

"No. I almost told him, but my mind was racing with everything he was telling me. At the time I wasn't for sure if he was my father. I'm still not completely sure."

"Hmm. I must confess that I had contemplated that the motive behind all this watch business was to get your gold."

"Yeah, I thought about that too. You should have been inside of his house. I'd say he has plenty enough treasure in that one room I was in to just about equal my one treasure in the bank."

<><><><>

Peter was happy to see the Azores as the ship approached. He and the whole crew were relieved when they saw no hostile ships in the harbor. Captain Gibson was in such a good mood that he allowed the crew to go ashore in shifts. Gibson declined Braganza's offer to stay at his cousin's house, but African John accepted.

The Braganza children were especially excited to see Brown and Peter again. The children had remembered the English words Brown had taught them. They were fascinated with African John's stories from his childhood.

Braganza's sister-in-law prepared a large meal for everybody. After that, she gave both Brown and Peter a pair of socks that she had made for them. She had just finished a new pair for her husband and gave them to John as a gift.

That afternoon, Braganza showed Peter and John the town. They also rode horses around the country side. Peter thoroughly enjoyed the Azores. He could easily imagine living their.

Throughout the day the Braganzas allowed the crew members to get free fruit from their store.

They invited Captain Gibson and the crew to dinner at their house and this time he accepted. All the crew who did not have to stay on board were at the Braganza's house. The men were grateful to eat in a regular house instead of a ship, or a pub. Several of the crew began to lead others in songs. Peter understood why the crew was so cheerful. These men spent so much time away at sea that they longed for their families, or wished they had one. Moments such as these were cherished.

Captain Gibson decided to stay in the Azores one more day to keep the crew's spirits up.

"Mr. Stewart, have you ever been up north?" Captain Gibson asked.

"Just as far as Savannah."

"Well then, you'll enjoy Philadelphia because that's where we're headed when we shove off here."

Even though Peter was in a hurry to get home he was excited about seeing Philadelphia.

Early the next morning Peter awakened from a dream. He dreamt that he was back home. In the dream he gave his mother the letter from the man who claimed to be his father. His mother burst into tears of happiness when she read it. Then there was a knock on the door. Peter peered out the window and saw that it was Mr. Monroe standing on the porch; only now he recognized him as his father. His mother screamed at him to let his father in, but Peter could not move. He just stood there looking at his father through the window.

<><><><>

Later that evening, Peter, African John, Captain Gibson and Brown had their last dinner with Braganza and his brother's family. The Braganza children were saddened to learn that Peter and his friends African John and Brown would be leaving the next morning. With Braganza interpreting, Peter promised to visit them again if he ever returned to England.

Peter was so excited about sailing home to America that he could hardly sleep. He was the first person to wake up that morning. A few minutes later Mrs. Braganza came into the kitchen to cook breakfast. Peter taught her some English while she cooked breakfast.

John had eaten an early breakfast so he could help the crew ready the ship. After breakfast, Brown and Peter said their good-byes to all the Braganzas. The crew and Captain Gibson were ready to embark when Brown and Peter boarded. A few minutes later Braganza came running down the dock. As soon as the gang plank was pulled in, Gibson barked out his familiar, "Anchors" and the anchors were hauled in. Peter did not bother looking back at the Azores as they pulled out to sea. He went down below, to look over their course to Philadelphia, with Braganza.

Peter did just about every kind of job imaginable during the next several days. He cleaned clothes, helped the cook, piloted the ship, and one afternoon Gibson even let him be the captain.

About a week after leaving the Azores they came upon another ship that was also heading west. Captain Gibson took out his spyglass to see what country it was from.

"Ah, I was right," Gibson said as he spied the ship. "It's a ship of immigrants. Probably from Germany."

He handed the spyglass to the men around him. Peter took a turn looking at the ship. The deck was full of families. They were all gathered together on the side nearest The Confidence so they could see. They waved and shouted words that meant nothing to Peter or the crew.

One time at dinner the discussion turned to beards. Most of the crew had beards and Captain Gibson suggested to Peter that he grow one. Peter had thought about growing a beard, but never tried it. The novelty of shaving had worn off a couple of years ago so Peter decided to raise a beard.

<><><><>

Much to Peter's surprise, the ship had only encountered three moderate rainstorms so far. They were one and one half days away from Philadelphia when they came upon a powerful storm. It was not as strong as the storm he battled on the way to Island Unknown, but still made him fearful. He was happy he had not talked his mother into going with him. Peter helped the helmsman steer the wheel as walls of water crashed onto the deck. One of the crew, named

Fletcher, was swept off his feet and thrown into one of
the masts. The man injured his arm and shoulder
badly. African John saw that he was in agony and
carried him down below.

It took about an hour to pass through the worst
of the storm. It continued to rain for another two
hours. After it stopped raining Peter went below to
change into dry clothes. He checked on Fletcher, or
Fletch, as the crew called him. Braganza and Brown
had put his arm in a sling.

"How's your arm, Fletch?" Peter asked as he
wrung water out of his hair.

"It's right bloody broken it is. That's about the
third time I've been knocked off me feet during a
storm."

"You better stay below next time, or else nail
your shoes to the deck."

Fletch laughed and then groaned in pain.

"I thought his shoulder was out of place when I
first saw him." Brown noted. "Braganza held him down
so I could put his shoulder back in place. I must say
that I was quite startled when his arm bent in half
when I started to put the shoulder back in place."

"The break nearly pierced his skin," Braganza
added. "Fletch gave quite a yell that sent Gibson
storming in. I'm surprised you did not hear it."

"No, it was too noisy on deck."

Chapter 8   Philadelphia

Peter was especially excited about reaching land again. By Braganza's calculations The Confidence was about twenty nautical miles away from land when Peter awakened. He decided to stay out on deck and help the crew so he could see the land. Brown came up on deck later and joined him. He began quizzing Brown about Philadelphia.

"It will be some time before we reach Philadelphia you know," Brown informed Peter. "It's not close to the coast like our town. We'll have to travel up the Delaware River. It's almost sixty miles from the ocean."

Peter did not care. He knew they were close to land. He could see the fishing vessels now as well as a couple of cargo ships.

By mid morning the vague, dark shape of the coastline appeared on the horizon. Captain Gibson told Peter to take a break so he could see the sights. Finally, their watery path narrowed as the ship moved into Delaware Bay. Brown joined Peter at the bow of The Confidence.

"It's quite different from Georgia, wouldn't you say, Peter?"

"It is," Peter answered. "It's also different from Liverpool. I sort of feel like I'm heading home. Guess that's because this is my country."

Fletch came out on the deck to get some fresh air and to feast his eyes on the land. Fletch had sailed to Philadelphia many times. He knew the names of all the coves, islands, and towns near the river.

Brown explained that the company's warehouse was at the mouth of the Schuylkill River. His brother, Charles, lived one half of a mile away.

Much to Peter's disappointment, their rate of speed had declined as they moved up the Delaware.

Just before sunset Captain Gibson ordered the helmsman to anchor the ship. Fletch told Brown and Peter that they were halfway up the river to Philadelphia at a place called Cohansey Cove.

That evening after supper Peter and African John had the first watch. Captain Gibson was uneasy about a small ship that was anchored fifty yards away.

It was now three hours after everyone had gone to bed. Peter and African John were talking about their parents when John suddenly put his hand across Peter's mouth. He looked out across the river towards the ship that Captain Gibson had been worried about. John started to rise.

"What is it?" Peter whispered.

John shook his head and covered his own mouth to silently tell Peter to keep quiet. Peter was just about to stand up when he was hit in the back of the neck. Men suddenly began pouring onto the deck in an attempt to take over the ship. Peter was so surprised that he never had time to notice the pain from whatever hit him. He yelled for Captain Gibson and then joined African John in trying to defend the ship from the howling marauders. Peter was struck repeatedly with sticks. He managed to grab one of the men around the waist and picked him up off the ground and ran towards the side of the ship with him and threw him overboard. Just as he turned to help African John he was hit in the side of his head with a large stick. Peter dropped to one knew and noticed the crew and Captain Gibson storming onto the deck from below. Gibson and Braganza both had guns. The pirates began jumping overboard when they saw the guns. One of the marauders had a gun. Just before he jumped overboard he tried to pull his pistol from his waistband. Before he could remove it the gun went off and he shot himself in the upper thigh. The man howled in pain before falling overboard into the river. The crew quickly ran to the side and cursed the men as they swam back to their boat.

Gibson looked over Peter and John's wounds. He ordered them to be taken down below. Gibson noticed Brown standing there wondering what all the commotion was about. He ordered him back down below deck as well. Peter was in a bit of shock, but he couldn't help but notice Gibson's tone of voice. He was in such a state of rage that Peter knew something was going to happen. As Brown and a crewman helped John and Peter below he heard some of the crew begging Captain Gibson to sink the pirates' ship. Peter and Brown were told to stay in their quarters. There was much commotion on deck and down below.

"My God man. What *happened* tonight?" A frantic Brown asked.

Peter began to feel the effects of his wounds. He felt tingles down both his arms. One side of his face felt hot. When he touched his face he noticed he was bleeding pretty badly.

"Those men from that ship down the river tried to sneak on board and steal our cargo. I was on deck talking with John and they attacked us. They were going to kill us."

Brown found a rag and began cleaning the blood from Peter's head and face.

Just then, the ship began lurching forward.

"We're moving? Why are we *moving*?" Brown asked.

Peter said nothing. The pain from his wounds was starting to get unbearable.

A crewman named Johnston entered the cabin and shut the door behind him.

"I want to know why we are moving? What's *happening* out there?" Brown pleaded.

"Please don't ask questions Mr. Brown," Johnston pleaded. "It will be over soon."

Peter knew exactly what was going to happening.

A few minutes later, gunshots began ringing out in the distance from somewhere off the port side.

Through the popping of gunshots, a loud explosion cut through the chaos. Brown jumped out of his seat.

"*Good God!* That sounded like a cannon. We've a *cannon?*"

Johnston said nothing.

During the next minute or two more thunderous explosions rang out. Then they heard the crew above deck cheering loudly.

They continued sailing up the river for perhaps an hour before dropping the anchors again.

There was a knock on the door. Johnston let Braganza in. Braganza looked at the back of Peter's neck and head.

"Just some bumps is all," Peter stated. "I stopped most of the hits with my arms. How's African John?"

"He is good. They hardly touched him."

Peter gave Braganza a serious look.

"Did it sink?"

Braganza nodded.

"Well I must say that is most unusual of a captain and his crew." Brown commented. "We should have informed the authorities."

"Captain Gibson *is* the authority when it comes to his ship, Mr. Brown," said Braganza. He shook his head and sighed loudly. "That is the way we do things. Captain Gibson would give his life to see to it that a shipment gets through."

Peter had a hard time moving his arms when he awakened the next morning. The back of his neck ached whenever he made any sudden movements. He accidentally rolled over and the side of his head felt like he was getting hit again. He let out a yelp of pain that woke up Brown. He felt the raised bump on the side of his head.

"Sorry I woke you. Made the mistake of trying to sleep on that knot on the side of my head. I won't be wearing a hat for a few days. Can't sleep on my back either."

After breakfast Peter went up on deck to see the sights of the Delaware River. Fletch was standing near the very mast that broke his arm.

"How's ye back?"

"My neck and my head" Peter corrected him. "They hit me with something right back here and got him on my head right here." Peter turned and showed Fletch the back of his neck and lifted his hair to show off the lump on the side of his head.

"You lucky it didn't crack ye skull. It was a rock that got your neck. I saw that rock before Captain Gibson threw it overboard. I'm telling you it was bigger than me fist it was. Didn't go too well for them. I heard three of them drowned. They said the one who shot his own leg made it to the other side. Dumb, but lucky that bloke was."

"Does this sort of thing happen a lot?"

"What, piratin'? Oh, maybe two or three times a year. Not like it did long time ago. Not much thievery on the water. Most of the time people try to steal things out of the warehouses."

Fletch looked over at Captain Gibson. He was checking the depth of the river.

"Gibson told us to keep quiet about last night. Just know that none of them thieves was killed by us." Fletch flashed his trademark toothless smile. "They just don't have a boat to get around in anymore."

As they continued up the river to Philadelphia they passed more cargo ships than they had seen during the whole journey to England. It was comforting to travel with land on either side.

Peter was impressed with Philadelphia as The Confidence nudged its way nearer and nearer to the city. After they docked at the warehouse Captain Gibson allowed the crew two nights in Philadelphia. They were free to go as they pleased. A couple of the crew had friends or family in town. It seemed that everyone but Peter and African John had some place to go in Philadelphia.

Captain Gibson asked Brown to find his brother
Charles at his store since the warehouse was locked.
Charles had his store a couple of streets inland.

Peter went with Brown to get his brother. Peter
had not liked Charles ever since he gave him the
watch two months earlier. He disliked him even more
now that he knew he had been paid to keep quiet
about the watch.

Charles displayed no emotion upon seeing his
brother. All he cared about was his shipment of
merchandise. He walked so fast to the warehouse that
Peter and Brown remained a good twenty feet behind.

As soon as he unlocked the warehouse Charles
waved to Captain Gibson as a message to start
unloading his cargo. Charles sighed heavily and looked
at his brother.

"I suppose you will be staying overnight."

"I can spend my nights aboard the ship so not
to inconvenience you."

Charles glanced at Peter.

"No, brother, *you* can stay at my house."

Peter understood that *he* was not welcome. He
would have declined if Charles had offered for him to
stay at his house. Peter realized that Charles's
relationship with his brother was strictly business.

Charles reached into his jacket and took out a
small pencil and notepad. He wrote something down
and handed the paper to his brother.

Brown looked at the paper. It was an address.

"What is this place? I thought you offered your
home for the night. Am I to stay at this address
instead?"

"I'm no longer at my previous residence. I
purchased another home eighteen months ago. That is
the address. Get your fisherman to help you transport
your bags there."

"A new house? You failed to mention that
information during our last conversation in
Brunswick."

"That's quite right. There was no need to inform you until now. Knock on the door and someone will assist you. I must return to my business."

Peter and Brown looked at one another.

"My sister in Liverpool and my brother in Savannah tell me everything that is happening in their lives no matter how trivial," Brown explained to Peter. "Charles, on the other hand, could move to Paris and fail to communicate that bit of information to me. It makes me wonder what else he has kept to himself.

"If you only knew about your dear brother," Peter thought to himself.

After the crew unloaded the cargo Brown went to get his luggage from the ship. Peter helped Brown carry one of his bags to Charles' house a few blocks from his store.

Brown and Peter stood at the front entrance to the home and looked it for a moment.

"Charles' business must be doing well judging by the size of the place," Peter said.

"Indeed, most impressive residence," was all Brown could say.

They noticed a young woman sweeping the porch as they walked up the sidewalk that led to the front door.

"Hmm, I can't believe my brother would ever open his wallet to pay for a housekeeper," Brown whispered. "Perhaps this young lady is paying off a debt from a purchase at Charles' shop?"

The young woman rested her broom against one of the massive front port columns. She seemed relieved to have visitors.

"Good afternoon, gentlemen."

"Afternoon to you, ma'am. I'm Richard Brown. My brother is Charles Brown. He has asked me to stay the night here. This is Mr. Stewart. He accompanied the ship to and from England."

"Oh *good*." She put down her broom. "Please come in and sit down." She looked at Peter. "Will you be staying as well, sir?"

Peter shook his head.

"I didn't know Mr. Brown had any siblings. He rarely talks about things outside of his store. It's rather dull here during the business hours. I'm so glad to have the company."

Brown was somewhat confused.

"How long have you worked for my brother, ma'am?"

The lady chuckled.

"Oh, I'm not the housekeeper. I'm *Mrs.* Brown. Charles and I married last year."

Brown glanced at Peter with embarrassment.

"Pardon me, madam. I had no idea... I just do not know what to say. Please accept my deepest apology."

Mrs. Brown smiled.

"It seems that Mr. Brown rarely talks with *you* either."

Brown nodded and tried to stifle a laugh.

"Quite true."

Peter stayed long enough to have a slice of pie before leaving. He really liked Mrs. Brown, but he could not understand why she would marry a man like Charles.

Peter walked along the docks to look at all the merchant ships. After a few minutes he spotted a familiar vessel- it was Captain Chester's ship, The Shiloh. Peter hurried back to The Confidence to see if the crew had finished unloading the cargo. Captain Gibson and Captain Chester were talking in front of the warehouse.

"Peter Stewart?" Captain Chester called. "Come here man!"

Peter shook hands with Chester.

"I heard Mr. Brown went to stay with his brother for a couple of days. You best tell him to be ready to leave at sunrise. We're not able to stay here an extra day. We need to get shipments to Charleston and Savannah before we stop at Brunswick. Then we need to get down to Nassau."

"It's been good sailing with you, Stewart," Captain Gibson said as he patted Peter on the shoulder. "We leave for New York in a couple of days and then we sail back to England. Perhaps we'll sail into your port sometime. That's up to the company, though."

Peter went back to Charles's house tell Brown about the new plans.

Peter was disappointed that crew of The Confidence would not be sailing to his home town. He wanted his mother and Andrew to meet the crew-especially African John, Braganza, and Captain Gibson. Peter kept feeling sorry that he was leaving his new friends. Braganza had taught him a lot about navigation and Portugal. Captain Gibson had taught him how to be a great leader. Most importantly, African John taught him about life.

Later, Peter helped the crew unload some cargo from The Confidence to Captain Chester's ship. By the time they finished, the men were thirsty so many of them went to their favorite tavern. Braganza was now reunited with his equally ambitious friend, Captain Chester. They talked about eventually serving together on the company's route to the Far East.

The Confidence's cook, Mr. Roberts, bought a goose to cook for the men who did not go into the city. All but four of the crew stayed to watch the ship. Mr. Roberts stayed long enough to cook the goose.

After supper, they went on deck to sit and talk. They were joined by a couple of deckhands from The Shiloh. A couple of the crew enjoyed their brand new smoking pipes they had bought from a shop near the docks. African John told some more stories about his life in Africa. Some of the stories were obviously myths, but all were interesting and enjoyable. Peter and African John stayed out on deck and continued talking long after the other crewmen had turned in. Peter told John about what happened to his father and about Mr. Monroe in Liverpool.

"What do you think I should do about all this, John?"

He thought for a moment.

"Peter, what I think does not matter. I will not tell you what to do. You are a man and you are in charge of your life. I know you will do what is good for you and your mother."

John looked up at the stars.

"It gets late and we leave in the morning. I would like to give you a gift. I have it with my things."

Peter followed John to the crew's quarters. John shared a small cabin with two other sailors who were still somewhere in the city. Peter noticed only two beds.

"There's three to a cabin. What happened to the third bunk?" Peter asked.

"I do not need it. Before I worked here I was on smaller ships. We slept on the floor. I got used to that. I choose this way. They try and get me to use the bunk but I give it back and tell them no."

"I'm going to see if the company can sail to Brunswick for one of the next shipments from England," Peter said. "I would like for you to see where I live and to meet my mother and cousin."

"That would be good. Maybe some day I can open a store in Philadelphia and you and your mother could visit me?"

John picked up a pillowcase off the floor. He used it to hold his belongings. He took out a necklace with an animal claw attached to it.

"I make this for you. It comes from my home." John said proudly.

Peter looked at the claw.

"Bear claw?"

"No, *lion* claw. The lion is strong like you and like me."

Peter quickly put on the necklace. He smiled.

"*Lion's* claw."

African John nodded and laughed.

"You should keep this. I wish I had a gift for you, John."

John laughed and pulled out a lion's claw necklace from inside his shirt.

"We have the same," John smiled. "No gift, Peter. You talk to me the same as Braganza and all the men who work on ship. That is enough."

"Well, even if the company can only come to Savannah I can sail up there so we can visit. I don't have a lot of friends back home. You're a good friend, John. I hope you can open that shop someday."

Chapter 9   Savannah and Andrew

Fletch awakened Peter early the next morning.

"Cap Chester over on The Shiloh says they will shove off in about an hour. You best fetch Mr. Brown right quick."

Peter quickly dressed and gathered his things and a couple items Brown had left. He was especially careful with his new suit and shoes. As he made his way up towards the deck African John popped his head out from his cabin.

"Good sailing with you, my friend," John said.

John and Peter shook hands and patted each other on the back. Peter took out his lion's claw necklace from underneath his shirt.

"Everyone back home will love to see this. You take care and we will visit again."

Peter took the belongings to Captain Chester's ship. Much to his surprise Braganza was standing next Chester.

"Are you going to navigate us south?"

"Oh no, I'm just saying farewell to my captain friend here. Be careful going out the river. Watch out for any thieves."

"Don't you worry about us," Captain Chester said. He turned to Peter. "Stewart, you can put your things in the cabin next to mine. It's the only one with an open door."

"Yes sir. I will run and get Mr. Brown."

"We weigh anchor in less than an hour.

Peter shook hands with Braganza.

"Tudo de bom, Braganza."

"Very good, Peter. All the best to you too."

Brown was having breakfast when Peter got to Charles's house.

"Ah, Peter, do you have time for breakfast?"

Peter took a quick look out the window. The sun had already risen.

"Captain Chester sent me to get you. We better get there. They weigh anchors in less than an hour."

Peter looked around the room.

"Oh, my husband is still asleep," Mrs. Brown said with a smile.

Peter and Brown had a brief, but enjoyable, conversation with Mrs. Brown. She almost cried as Brown and Peter left. It was obvious that she was miserable living with Charles. Peter and Brown hurried to the ship.

"I do hope I am not holding up the departure. Is Captain Chester angry?"

"No, he'll be ready to leave in a bit, but he's not mad at all."

Brown glanced back at his brother's house. Mrs. Brown was still standing on the front walk watching them walk away. She waved enthusiastically and bid Peter and Brown a safe voyage.

"Quite a shame that poor girl. Twenty-two years of age she is. It's been some time since I was so embarrassed. I just naturally assumed she was the housekeeper. It was nearly as I expected. She was an indentured servant and Charles paid her debt. He essentially purchased a bride for himself. I can not believe Charles neglected to inform me that he acquired a new house *and* a bride."

Captain Gibson was standing on the dock talking with Captain Chester.

"Thought I would see the good captain off. Until next time, Mr. Brown. It was good having you on The Confidence, Mr. Stewart."

"Perhaps Brunswick could be your first stop in the near future," Brown said. "Mr. Stewart met with Mr. Monroe whilst we were in Liverpool."

"Oh, well that would be the man to make that change," Gibson said. "It'll be him or Mr. Reece. Whoever it is I sail where I'm ordered to."

Peter helped Brown put his belongings in their cramped quarters below. They returned to the deck to watch the crew ready the ship for departure.

"You may have to meet me in Brunswick next time, Captain Chester," Gibson hollered. Captain smiled and saluted to Captain Gibson down on the dock.

Brown and Peter both flinched as Chester barked out his first orders to his crew.

"I've forgotten what lungs the man has," remarked Brown.

"I heard we have a quick stop in Charleston before we get to Savannah," Peter said. "I sure am ready to see Mother and Andrew. I know The Shiloh is a lot smaller, but at least she's faster than The Confidence."

"The Shiloh is much smaller," Brown noted. "We didn't have to stay overnight on her last time we were on this ship. That's an awfully small cabin we will be sleeping in. It's hardly large enough for one man."

Late in the afternoon they passed the small ship that Gibson's crew had cannon-balled the night before. The ship had taken on water and was resting on the bottom of the river. Most of the deck was still above water. Gibson's crew had not obliterated the ship, but had prevented it from ever sailing again. The crew of The Shiloh all gathered on the side closest to the sunken ship for a better look. Many of the men joked about it.

By nightfall they were in the Atlantic Ocean sailing south. Peter could not wait to see Andrew again. He wanted to tell him all about his meeting with Mr. Monroe and the attack on the ship in the river as well as his experiences he had in the Azores and with the crew of The Confidence. He frequently took out his lion's claw necklace and felt the long claw attached to the string of leather.

Peter found that if he stayed on one side he could be comfortable enough to sleep. The bunk in the cabin took up much of the space. It was awkward sleeping so close to Brown. Right before Peter fell asleep he was startled by a vibration sound coming from the side of the cabin nearer the stern.

"Brown, are you awake?" Peter called out.

"Well, I was until that dreadful crunching sound awakened me."

"We don't have an engine on this boat." Peter remarked.

"Not on this boat. She's driven by the wind." Brown put his ear to the wall. "It does have a rhythm to it like an engine, but much slower."

Peter and Brown were awakened several times throughout the night by the strange sound. It went away entirely just before sunrise

Captain Chester's crew was different from Gibson's. Every crew member on Chester's ship had been born in Pennsylvania. Although they were friendly towards Brown and Peter none of them bothered to get to know them like the crew of *The Confidence*. Peter figured it was because they were out at sea so much that they were more lonesome for friendship.

The trip to Charleston was uneventful. Peter was interested in seeing what Charleston looked like. Brown joined him out on deck.

"Have you been to Charleston before?" Brown asked. "It's not too far from Brunswick and Savannah."

"Never been here. I think someone I knew when I was a kid moved up here."

The Shiloh moved up the harbor and looked for a place to dock. Peter and Brown nearly had to cover their ears over Captain Chester's thunderous orders. They docked between two ships. One of them was being unloaded.

"I'm going to the cabin, Peter," Brown abruptly said. "I'll not witness this."

Peter didn't understand until he noticed the activity on the small ship docked behind them. Peter called Captain Chester away from his duties.

"Excuse me, captain, but is that boat unloading slaves?" Peter questioned. "I thought it was against the law to bring slaves to our country?"

Captain Chester looked at the people being unloaded in chains.

"It's against the law to bring in *new* slaves."

"Well, how do they know they didn't come from Africa?" Peter asked.

"I'm sure they got some way of doing it. People still smuggle slaves in. They're probably taking them to the slave mart for auction." Captain Chester could tell how much it bothered Peter. "We're gonna get this shipment unloaded and be on our way as soon as we can. That right there is one job this captain wouldn't do. Things are different down here then back home in Philadelphia. They put an end to slave sales a few years ago. Go walk up and down the dock here and you'll be lucky to find a dockhand who isn't a slave. I have to be careful who I say this to, but it's like my daddy used to say, 'It may not be breaking the law, but it breaks the law of ain't right.'"

Peter looked up and down the dock. Chester was right. Most of the workers were slaves.

"Ain't right is a good way to put it, Captain. I'm gonna head back to my quarters."

<><><><>

Brown was lying on the bunk when Peter went inside their cabin. Peter sat down on the edge of the bunk.

"Most uncivilized activity," Brown scoffed. "People treated like farm animals."

"Captain Chester said they passed laws up north to stop all that. Guess your brother Charles doesn't have to see much of it."

"Peter, I do not want to offend your patriotism, but that was one apprehension which prevented me from opening a store in this country particularly in the southern region. I had looked into a franchise in Rhode Island or Connecticut. I was reluctant when Mr. Reece kept suggesting Brunswick. He took advantage of my close relationship to my brother in Savannah. As

I said, do not be offended. I am happy in Brunswick and enjoy the customers and the friendship of your family. The slavery is something I can never be comfortable with."

"Some of the old timers told me about some slaves they were taking to a plantation over on St. Simons Island. They said the slaves took over the ship. Rather than be captured and made slaves they all killed themselves by drowning."

"Senseless," Brown scoffed. "Utter senselessness."

"I'd like to know how they passed them laws up in Philadelphia. Maybe Brunswick could do the same."

"You know the plantation owners hold a great deal of power," Brown added. "It takes a lot of people. The will of the people can be stronger than the money of a few."

Peter and Brown continued to talk about what they had seen on the docks for over an hour.

Later that night Peter and Brown had been asleep only a few minutes when the deep, vibrating sound started up again,

"Oh, is there no respite from this unholy cacophony?" Brown wailed.

"I never heard some of those words you just said, but I'm gonna guess you're tired of that noise that keeps us up at night."

"Bravo, Mr. Stewart. Shall we continue our discussion on slavery until peace prevails?"

<><><><>

Brown was excited about seeing his brother and his family in Savannah. He had always been close to Henry. They were best friends as children and visited frequently until Henry moved away from England to open his company store. Henry had his store right on the Savannah River. He and his wife and two children lived above their store.

It was late at night when the ship docked at Henry's store. Brown reluctantly went around back to awaken his brother. After several minutes the glow of a lantern could be seen from inside the store. Henry was still in his night clothes when he came out to talk to Captain Chester.

Unlike Charles, Henry was not immediately concerned with his share of the shipment. He welcomed Captain Chester, the crew, and Peter. Later, he insisted that everyone call him Henry. Mrs. Brown also came down to the dock to greet everyone. She offered everyone coffee and asked if anyone was hungry.

Much to Peter's surprise Henry persuaded Captain Chester to spend the night in his home. Peter had to share a room with Chester. Every one was tired and went to bed after a brief conversation. Peter was delighted to, once again, sleep on a regular bed on solid ground. He was looking forward to a good night's sleep until Captain Chester fell asleep. Captain Chester had, without a doubt, the loudest voice that Peter had ever heard. It was only fitting that he would also have a loud snore. Peter realized what the grinding noise he and Brown kept hearing at night in their cabin. It was Captain Chester's snoring. It made sense that the noise started about the time they went to sleep and stopped around an hour before sunrise. Peter managed to get about an hour of sleep that night. He thanked Heaven every time Chester would roll over onto his stomach. This allowed Peter to get in a few minutes of precious sleep before Chester rolled back over, and again, filled the room with the awful noise. Peter felt helpless because there was nowhere else to sleep. The children were asleep in the parlor. It really didn't matter where Peter slept because there was no place in the house where the snore could not be heard. He felt he could not do anything because the man was the captain. At one point Peter yelled at Chester to, "Stop that God-awful noise." This only managed to stop the snoring for a few seconds.

Luckily for Peter, Captain Chester woke up about an hour early. Peter kept his eyes partially closed and pretended to be asleep. Chester carefully dressed and left the room without as much as a sound.

"*Now* he decides to be quiet?"

Peter finally got out of bed when Henry knocked on the door and announced that his breakfast was getting cold.

"Were you able to get any sleep?" Peter asked.

Brown shook his head.

"It wasn't much different than on the ship," he said. "Now we know what, or should I say who, kept us awake. Henry and his family also suffer from a lack of sleep. My niece and nephew thought a giant was sawing the house in half."

"I wonder if he kept the neighbors awake?" Peter joked.

Brown laughed. "At least the crew probably got a good night's sleep for a change."

Peter was in a rotten mood from the lack of sleep. There had been too many nights of little sleep and he was fed up with it. Now that he was close to Brunswick, all he wanted to do was get Andrew and head for home.

Brown and Henry were having an amusing conversation when Peter went into the kitchen for breakfast. They were reminiscing about a childhood experience. Peter could not help but notice the similarities between the two Browns.

"Henry, I need to get word to my cousin Andrew that I'm back. Remember, he took my boat up the river?"

"The river is the fastest way, but I'm afraid all I have is a row boat." Henry thought a moment. "You may certainly use my horses and wagon to retrieve your cousin."

Peter wasted no time. He knew that the sooner he got Andrew the sooner he could get back home. Peter and one of the deck hands hitched up the horses and he was off to find them. Peter had visited Aunt Martha and Andrew only two or three times so he vaguely knew the way. Andrew and his family lived on a small farm next to a large plantation.

Peter knew he was in the right place when he got to the plantation. Andrew's place was the next house. Aunt Martha came out on the porch to greet him as soon as she heard the wagon approach. It had been a few years since she last saw him so she did not recognize him at first. "Can I help you sir?"

Peter jumped down from the wagon.

"Sir? What do you mean, sir? It's me, Peter...your *nephew*."

She immediately blushed with embarrassment.

"Dear Lord, it is you. You've gotten so big I can hardly believe it. And you have a beard too. My, you know you look just like your father when he married your mother."

Aunt Martha led Peter into the house and brought him some water. Peter looked around anxiously.

"Is Andrew out working or something?"

Aunt Martha immediately dropped her constant smile.

"Ah, no. Not anymore."

"Well, where is he?"

She led Peter to a bedroom. Andrew was there asleep. A young woman was sitting next to the bed just watching Andrew sleep. She was surprised to see Peter.

"This is Emily. Her papa owns the plantation."

"I think I remember you," Peter said. "We were kids and Andrew took me over to your house to play."

Just then, Andrew began stirring and awakened.

"You have a *visitor* today," Emily told him. She talked to him like he was a little child.

Andrew struggled to sit up. Peter was shocked at Andrew's condition. He had lost a lot of weight and had dark circles around his eyes.

Andrew rubbed his eyes and tried to focus in on Peter's face. He sat there and looked at Peter for a moment before he realized who it was.

"Hey, is it who I think it is?" Andrew said in a feeble voice. "It's Peter." Andrew turned to Emily. "Look, its Peter. He finally came back from England." Andrew laughed a bit before being overcome with a cough. "Would you look at that beard, Mother? Peter's a real sailor now."

Aunt Martha took Emily by the hand.

"Let's leave Andrew alone for awhile so he can talk with his cousin."

Emily seemed reluctant to go. She and Andrew gazed into each other's eyes for a moment before she followed Aunt Martha out of the room.

"You probably seen a lot of strange things over there in England."

Peter nodded his head in reply. He could not believe Andrew's physical condition.

"Anything exciting happen?"

"Well, we sunk a ship a few nights ago." Peter said as he stared in disbelief at Andrew."

"Sunk a ship? You'll have to tell me about that."

Andrew was ignoring the subject at hand.

"What *happened* to you Andrew? You look like Death itself has gotten a hold of you."

Andrew smiled and laughed before having another brief coughing attack.

"I look bad do I? You should've seen me a few days back. They thought I was a dead man fer sure."

"Well, what's got you to looking like this?" A puzzled Peter asked.

"The doctor from Savannah said I got what's killing a lot of people in town and over in some towns around here. I forget what he called it cause I had a fever. All I remember was feeling bad a couple days after I had got back here from taking your mother back to... that place where you live." Andrew took a sip of water from a cup on the nightstand. "I guess I'm lucky cause I'm gonna be all right. If it weren't for

Emily watching over me and prayin' I'd be dead and buried now." Andrew looked around. "Emily? Where's Emily?"

"It's alright. She and your mother just left the room so we could talk."

"Oh. I thought something happened to her. She saved my life. If it weren't for her I'd be dead and buried."

"Andrew, you just said that."

"I did? Oh, well, I had that fever and it messed me up some." He reached over and put the cup back on the table and closed his eyes. "I don't know if I could live without her now, Peter."

Peter did not say anything. It was apparent that Andrew and Emily were strongly in love. Andrew was in no condition to travel and Peter doubted that he would want to return to Georgia.

Andrew drifted off to sleep so Peter let Andrew rest.

Emily immediately took her place again beside the bed.

"Andrew's only been home for a couple days," Aunt Martha said. "Emily's family paid for a doctor to come treat him in their guesthouse. They made it into a little hospital just for him. Nobody could be around him when he was contagious. Emily sat outside his window and read to him and sang songs. You could see him perk up a little every time he heard her voice. Most people who get that sickness don't make it. He just kept getting sick to his stomach and his skin turned yellow. I thank God Andrew is gonna be well soon."

"I'm worried that Mother got the fever too. There's some folks back home that have died from that fever."

"Andrew was back for several days before he started to go down. I think he got it working out in the fields."

"The ship I came in on is leaving this afternoon for Brunswick. I borrowed that wagon to get here. I need to let them know I'll be sailing back in my boat."

"Emily, can get one of the help to follow you in their carriage?" Aunt Martha asked. "You will stay the night at least?"

"Yes ma'am, I'm anxious to get back home, but I can stay here a night."

<><><><>

Captain Chester was ready to leave when he got back to Henry's house. Peter thought about sailing back on The Shiloh, but then he would have to wait to get the Free Spirit II.

"Captain Chester, I'm sailing back on my own boat. My cousin had the fever, but it looks like he'll get better. I came to get my bag and things. I also need to take care of some business here."

Brown and Peter talked with Captain Chester and Henry and his family for awhile. The topic of conversation eventually turned to Mr. Monroe. Chester's eyes widened

"Hold on a minute here. You *know* the owner do you?"

Peter really did not know how to answer that question.

"Well, I suppose...I talked with him at his request. Mrs. Carey still owns half of it."

"If he requested you then you must be pretty important to him. You could tell him I'd be good for the route to China." Chester slapped Peter on the back.
"How bout it?"

Peter shrugged his shoulders.

"I'm not sure I'll see the man again. If I do I'll tell him you should be a captain on the China route." Peter thought for a moment. "And I'll tell him Braganza would be a great navigator for you too."

"I shall see you as soon as I return from England," Henry said. "It will be my turn to oversee the next shipment. I'll make sure the ship sails straight to Brunswick."

"Oh, I'm glad to hear that," Peter said. "I sure hope its The Confidence."

"Whatever ship it is I'll be here waiting to take the shipment to your brother Charles up in Philadelphia," Captain Chester said.

Chester smiled widely as he headed back to The Shiloh to ready it for departure. Henry noticed a couple walk into his store so he excused himself. Peter said goodbye to Henry's wife and their two children.

Now that they were alone Peter told Brown discussed Andrew's situation.

"Andrew's got a new life here now," Peter told him. "His cousins and his mother are here. He can settle down and become a farmer if he wants to, or he'll probably oversee that plantation. Most of all, he's got Emily now."

Brown was sympathetic, but realistic.

"I've found that some things are meant to be, Peter. Andrew grew up in a farming family. Perhaps that is his life's calling. Emily might also be in his destiny as well."

"Peter, Captain Chester can take my portion of the shipment back home," Brown interjected. "I can sail back with you on your boat."

"Thanks for the offer, Brown. You really need to be there. Just check on Mother for me. Andrew got that fever and I'm still worried that she could have gotten it too. My aunt wants me to stay the night. I will be off tomorrow at first light. Right now I need to visit the bank here before I go back to Andrew's place. Those were my mother's orders."

Peter climbed into the Lumley's carriage. It was similar to the ones he had ridden in back in England. They had removed the glass windows for the summer. Peter started talking to the driver. He was of African descent with graying hair and wrinkled face.

Peter learned that Winston had been a driver for the Lumleys for around ten years. Before that he was in charge of the gardens around the main house of the plantation. Winston was born in Barbados and he and his family were sold to the Lumley family when he was a boy. Peter learned that most of the children were separated from their parents when they were sold.

Peter found it difficult again to speak with Andrew. He was still not himself and spoke mainly about Emily. Peter could tell that Emily felt threatened by him being there. She was probably worried that he would take Andrew back to Brunswick to live when he got better.

Peter spent the evening visiting with his Aunt Martha.

"I guess Andrew won't be traveling for awhile," Peter stated.

"It's going to take some more time until he gets his strength back. I imagine to you he looks pretty bad. He really has gotten a lot better. If you could have seen him a little over a week ago you would be asking me to call the undertaker."

Aunt Martha straightened her hair with her hands and Peter realized his mother does the same thing. Peter wanted to tell her about Mr. Monroe, but decided not to because of all she had been through with Andrew.

"What will you do for a deck hand, Peter?"

"I don't know. I'll work alone I suppose until Andrew comes back."

Aunt Martha did not say anything, but Peter could read the doubt in her eyes.

Peter had another night of little sleep. He kept thinking about Andrew. Peter had been so happy and hoped they would always be fishermen together. The more Peter thought about it the more he realized that maybe Andrew was better off here. His mother needed him and he needed to be there to help with the farm. Peter got out of bed and checked in on Andrew. He expected to see Emily at his bedside, but she had gone home. He thought about all that Emily had done to help nurse Andrew back to health.

"I don't think a team of mules can pull you apart from that Emily," he whispered.

Chapter 10 Home Again

For the first time in two months Peter began to see familiar coastline as he sailed past the Tybee Island Light Station.

The closer he got to home the more Peter began thinking about his mother and Monroe's letter. Peter decided that he would tell her as soon as possible.

Later that evening Peter was about an hour away from home. He started scanning the horizon looking to see if any of the fishermen were late coming in. He realized that he would be out fishing in a couple of days, only without Andrew.

It was just after sunset when he docked at his house. It was very comforting for Peter to see that everything was just how it was when he left. He carefully carried his new suit and shoes with him to the house. As soon as he stepped onto the front porch he was met by a barking dog. It was so dark that Peter had not even seen the dog. He tried to pet it, but it snapped at him. Peter's mother came out to see what the noise was about. Peter was standing in dim light so she did not recognize him.

"Who are you? What are you doing on my porch?"

Peter moved closer until he was fully illuminated by the lamp his mother was carrying. She crouched down and restrained the dog because it was about to start biting Peter.

"Well, I said what do you..."

"It's *me*, Mother." Peter interrupted.

"Peter?" She scrutinized his face. "You have a *beard*. You're back home!"

Peter squeezed past the snarling dog and into the house. He and his mother hugged for awhile.

"Where'd that dog come from?"

"He's supposed to be a gift for you."

"Well, I guess he'll have to get used to me. I thought he was gonna tear into my legs out there."

Peter and his mother went inside and sat down at the kitchen table.

"You brought back a suit I see?

Peter quickly went to hang it up in his wardrobe.

"I thought you'd never get home." She looked around the room. "It hasn't been the same around here. You have any problems at sea?"

"No, not too many problems I guess. Nothing but a storm or two."

"I saw they unloaded things for Mr. Brown last night," Mother said. "That ship left this morning before I woke up. Mr. Brown came by and said you would be here tonight or tomorrow most likely."

She touched his face.

"I didn't know you with this beard. You look a lot like your father."

Peter almost took the letter out of his bag, but he decided to show her in the morning.

"How was Martha? Well,... wait a minute." Peter's mother went to look out the window towards the dock. "Where's Andrew? Is he still out on the boat or something?"

Peter sighed heavily.

"No, Mother. Andrew was very sick when I went to get him from his house. He had been sick with what a lot people in Savannah have been dying from. I was worried that maybe you had gotten it."

"Oh, I heard about that fever from some people in town," she interrupted. "It was really bad back there in 1820. I knew some people in Savannah who died from the fever. They think it's from the mosquitoes."

"Well, Andrew's gonna pull through, thank God."

"Well that's a relief. Are you going to sail up to Savannah to get him when he's better?"

"I don't think he's gonna come back, Mother. He and the plantation owner's daughter are sweethearts; real sweethearts."

"Oh, I see, one of the Lumley girls." She patted his head. "It looks like your going to be the busiest fisherman in Georgia until you can get a new partner."

"Yeah, maybe it's the best place for Andrew. It's really not fair to Aunt Martha. I'm not going to worry about that for awhile. Right now I just want to enjoy being home."

Peter and his mother talked for an hour then Peter went to bed.

He had no trouble getting to sleep now that he had finally gotten home and was in his own bed. That night Peter had the same strange dream he had on the ship from England. He and his mother are inside their parlor when they hear a knock on the door. Peter, again, looks out the window and sees Mr. Monroe on the porch. Peter tries to open the door, but this time, his mother forbids him to open it. Just then, he hears a familiar voice from outside. "Let us in Peter. It's all *true*." It is Grandpa. Peter quickly pulls back the curtains. Grandpa is standing there dressed in a fine suit. He has that familiar grin upon his face that Peter had grown up with. Peter ignores his mother and unlocks the door. Just then, Grandpa and Monroe vanish. Peter's mother begins to cry, "Why did you do this to me Peter?" She pleads. "Why did you bring him back when you know he would leave again?"

The dream became too emotional for Peter so he ended it by waking up. He was surprised to find himself in his own bedroom. He still felt the rocking motion from being on a ship for so long. Peter had awakened a couple of hours later than normal. His mother had been keeping his breakfast warm. Peter ate breakfast and retrieved the letter from the man who claimed to be his father. The dream had prompted Peter to explain everything to his mother. He told her a little about the Azores and Philadelphia before telling her about what happened in Liverpool. Peter took out the watch and placed it on the table.

"I went to England with Mr. Brown to find the man who sent this watch."

Mrs. Stewart picked up the watch.

"I knew that, son. Did you find him? Did he say how he got it?"

Peter took a deep breath.

The man who sent the watch owns half the company that Mr. Brown gets his merchandise from. He is an American and he gave me a letter to give to you."

"A letter for *me*? Are you sure?" She looked at the folded letter as Peter handed it to her. "Well, just who is this man?"

"That's what I want you to tell me. He's known in England as Mr. Monroe, but he says he's *John Stewart*."

Mother did not say anything, but she had a worried look upon her face.

"This man sent for me while I was staying at Brown's sister's house in Liverpool," Peter continued. "He says he never found Island Unknown and was too ashamed to come back." Peter got up out of his chair and started walking towards the back door. "He sure knew a lot of things, Mother, but I was too young to remember his face. I'll leave you alone awhile." Peter opened the door and started to step outside. "Please read that letter."

Peter went into town to say hello to his friends that were not fishermen. He dropped by Brown's store to tell him that he gave his mother the letter. While he was there he told Robert Potter to spread the word that he needed someone to work as a deck hand. Potter assured him that he had a couple of people in mind.

Peter gave his mother a good two hours to study the letter. He decided to reattach his fishing nets and to check the *Free Spirit II* over.

The new dog had already stopped barking at Peter and was starting to become friendly. Peter did not know what to name the dog. He really did not seem like the sea-fairing type of dog like Captain was. The dog did have large, sharp teeth so Peter thought he might call him Shark.

After he finished checking over the boat he went to find his mother. She was out back feeding the chickens.

"Well, is the letter real?"

Mother nodded her head.

"It's him all right. There's things in there that only he and I knew." She turned and looked Peter in the eye. "Did you actually see this Mr. Monroe write the letter?"

"No. He pulled it out of a drawer. It was already sealed up."

She closed the door to the chicken coop. "Well, I don't know who wrote it because your father could hardly read or write."

"That's what he said," Peter interrupted. "He said he couldn't read, but the man who used to own the company taught him to read and write. He gave him half the company when he died."

"What about his face? Did you get a long look at him?"

"Well, yeah; we talked almost two hours. We sat about four feet apart."

Mother was beginning to get excited.

"Did you see a small mole near his right ear?"

"A mole?" Peter squinted his eyes and tried to remember. "I don't remember seeing anything like that, but there could have been. I don't know."

Peter's mother was visually disappointed.

"Then there's only one way to know if Mr. Monroe is telling the truth- I'll have to see what he looks like for myself."

Peter and his mother went inside to prepare lunch. Peter continued the conversation as he helped his mother.

"You may never get to see Mr. Monroe. Mr. Brown said he won't be sailing to Liverpool for another eight months or so."

"Oh I'm not planning to sail to England. You know I can't stand to be out there in the ocean. It's hard enough for me to ride in a boat to Savannah. No, I'm saying that if Mr. Monroe is really John then he'll come here looking for you."

Peter had been trying to be realistic about the whole matter. He was relieved to see that his mother was too.

"What will you do if he *does* come back here? What if it really *is* him?"

"I don't know, son. It has been so long that I've gotten used to the life of a widow."

"I don't know what I'd do either," Peter confessed. "I grew up hearing great things about my father from everybody in town. If Monroe is him then I don't know what to think."

Mother nodded in agreement.

"I never told you, but a part of me has always felt that he was alive somewhere. Your Grandpa felt the same. You know, I think that Grandpa urged you to find Island Unknown to see if there was any trace of your father. He never cared about that treasure. I remember Grandpa telling me one time that he figured John never came back purely out of pride."

The next morning at church the pastor welcomed Peter and Brown back from England. The congregation surprised them with a pot luck dinner in their honor. Peter had not felt so proud since he returned from finding the treasure on Island Unknown.

Peter had never thought about it, but many of the children in town looked up to him. They were full of questions about England, the Azores, and

Philadelphia. Two boys even volunteered to work for Peter if he could convince their teacher to let them quit school. The children and many of the adults at the dinner asked Peter to again tell them about his experiences in finding the treasure. They wanted to know all about Island Unknown. Peter was asked that question at least a couple times a month. He always said that it was a place nobody should go to.

Peter, Brown and Mother drove home that afternoon loaded with food.

"Such a thoughtful group of people," Brown remarked. "I was quite touched."

"See, you really have a home here now, Brown," Peter commented. "Did you see Leech Myers dance a jig for me? Course he waited until he was outside the church to do it. Did know about that surprise dinner?" Peter asked his mother.

Mother smiled.

"I'll admit to knowing about the dinner, but believe me son, it was their idea. All our friends and neighbors here love you like a favorite son or brother. That goes for you too, Mr. Brown."

Peter thought for a moment.

"I guess I have made a name for myself around here. Do you know this was the first time when the older folks didn't tell me a story about how great my father was? Come to think of it; his name was never even mentioned the whole time." Peter looked at his mother. He did not know if she wanted him mentioning his father what with the possibility of him still being alive. Peter read no negative reaction in her face so he continued. "I'll tell you mother; this has been a day that I'll never forget. For the first time in my life I feel like I'm Peter Stewart and not John Stewart's son. I'm my own man now."

Mrs. Stewart took her son's arm.

"You've been a man for some time now. Soon you'll find a woman that you'll want to marry and you'll be moving into a new house to start your own family. There's at least three nice young ladies at church."

"Andrew beat me on that race. Not that I was running. I expect I will someday, but I'll always live here in this town." Peter gave Mother a kiss on the cheek. "I just hope I marry a woman like you."

Chapter 11 New Deck Hands?

It had been a couple of days since Peter returned from his trip. He was so eager to get back to his normal routine that he decided to fish alone. It was strange being aboard his boat after living on such large ships for the past weeks. As expected, Peter had a difficult time working alone. He missed having Andrew there to share the burden. He also missed the company and conversations that he and Andrew had.

Peter managed to catch about half the average that he and Andrew usually caught. Even though Peter had tried to stay active on his trip to England his muscles tired easily under the workload. He was embarrassed when he docked at Mr. Milton's fish market.

"Well, I can see by the look on your face you're not too pleased with your catch," Milton said. "I heard you were back from England without Andrew. I sent the word out, but so far none of the captains can spare a deckhand right now. I'll keep trying."

"Thank you. I'll try and spread the word out too. Right now all I've got is some little boys from church willing to help me."

Peter awakened the next day with a very sore back. He was still determined to try working alone again. Just as he was leaving the house the new dog came up to greet him.

"You want to go fishin' with me, Shark?"

The dog followed him out to the pier so Peter put him on the deck of the *Free Spirit II*. Peter got a kick out of watching Shark experience his first boat ride. After Shark was able to maintain his balance he began barking. He barked at the water, the fish that Peter caught as well as the other fishing boats. After three hours of Shark's barking and a painful backache Peter decided to quit early and head for home.

Peter was desperate to get somebody to fill in for Andrew, either temporarily, or permanently. He went to Brown's store to see if Potter had found anybody to work with him.

Potter was eager to talk to Peter when he arrived at the store.

"Hey, I found you a deck hand today, Peter," Robert said proudly.

"Good. Good. Who is he and when can he start?" Peter said. He was too tired to build up Potter's ego.

"Well, actually it's *two* people."

"Ah, even better. What two people?"

"Uh, my neighbors, the Moore boys," Potter said rather reluctantly.

"Aren't they a couple of drunks?"

"Oh no, they don't drink when they're working. They sweared they would work hard until Andrew came back from Savannah."

Peter tried to think for a moment about who else he could get to work with him. He was too tired to think so he told Potter to tell the Moores to be at his dock at 5:30 the next morning.

Peter had heard the Moore boys were lazy, but he figured the two of them together might be able to do the work of one decent deck hand.

James and John Moore were fraternal twins about thirty years old. James had frizzy brown hair and John had straight blonde hair. They were quite a bit bigger than Peter so he thought they should be able to lift larger loads of fish. Neither one of the Moore boys had ever been to school a day in his life because their father forbid it. Since none of their family had ever been educated they spoke in broken English. Their father had a small plot of land that he farmed until he died some five years earlier. James and John let the fields become overgrown with weeds because they hated farming. They supported themselves and their mother by working odd jobs in and around town.

Peter knew he was in for another hard day when the Moores never showed up for work. Peter waited until 6:30 before riding over to their place.

As expected, Peter found them home asleep- on the roof of their house. Peter had heard some stories about how strange the Moores were, but until he saw them up there on the roof snoring away on mattresses with complete bedding he realized just how true some gossip can be.

Peter got off his horse and climbed up the ladder they had leaning against the roof.

"Hey, Moores! Wake up!" he yelled. "You're over an hour late for work."

The Moores laughed and then slowly climbed down the ladder.

"Oh boy, we gonna work for the treasure man," one of the Moores said as he held the ladder steady for his brother.

Peter was already disgusted in their attitudes. They were not even apologetic at all. In fact, they thought being late to work was funny.

After waiting another twenty minutes for the Moores to get dressed they finally left for work. Peter noticed the mattresses and blankets still on the roof.

"Aren't you going to get that bedding down off the roof?"

James looked up at the mattresses and shook his head.

"Naw, Mister Peter, we just leave that up thar."

"But what if the wind blows the sheets off, or it rains?"

"We puts rocks on top of dem so's they don't blow off, Mister Peter," John cut in. "Besides, Ma will git em' down if it come a rainin'."

"We's leavin' to work for Mister Peter, Ma!" James yelled. "He's the treasure man, you know."

"Shutup!" was Ma's answer.

Peter looked up towards the sky and shook his head.

"Why did you have to go and get sick, Andrew?" Peter asked silently.

James and John climbed on an old horse and trotted alongside Peter.

"What were you two doing sleeping on the roof?"

"Oh we always sleep like dat," James answered.

"Heck yeah, it's too blamed hot down in da house," John added.

After they boarded the *Free Spirit II* Peter thought he should get a few things straight with the Moores.

"We're late so we may have to stay out a little longer. Now, have either of you worked as a deck hand before?"

"No sir Mister Peter," James and John answered simultaneously.

"You can call me Peter. I'm not special or anything." Peter went over and weighed anchor. "Look, this fishing job is real easy to do. It's just hard work is all."

"We's ready to work, Mister Peter," James said as he turned to his brother for confirmation.

"Yep, we's ready Mister Peter."

"Just call me *Peter*," he said. Peter wasn't sure if the Moores understood what he was saying.

Peter had thought that working with his dog, Shark, was a disaster, but he would have gladly welcomed the dog back onboard to replace the Moore boys. John quit working after two hours because it was too hot for him. James talked and sung so loudly that Peter was sure he scared most of the fish away. When James was not singing he was arguing with his brother. The two constantly bickered back and forth. Peter had a terrific headache from listening to the Moore's arguments. They argued over everything no matter how trivial it was.

John sat in the shade of the cabin doorway while James was at the helm, steering The *Free Spirit II*. While Peter was tending to the nets when James and John actually started wrestling on the deck. Peter had had enough. He barely maintained his cool as he separated the two and shoved James into the cabin. He sent John to the bow of the ship.

"But it's too blamed hot out here in the sun," John complained. "Why can't James sit out here, Mister Peter?"

"Because he talks too much. And quit calling me *Mister Peter*!"

Peter pulled up the nets and headed for shore. Before he even delivered his tiny load of fish to Mr. Milton he decided to drop off the Moores at his pier.

"We can git here real early t'mornin', Mister Peter," James said innocently as he stepped onto the pier.

"Yes sir. We'll git our Ma to wake us up, Mister Peter," John added.

Peter shook his head in disgust.

"Neither one of you worked a day's wages, but I'm gonna be a gentleman and pay you in full."

The Moores looked at each other and smiled.

"You gonna pay us with some of that treasure you done found on dat ghost island?" James asked as he hitched up his pants.

Peter sighed. "I need somebody who can work the way I want them to work. I'll give the money to Potter later so you can have it by the weekend."

"Thank ye, Mister Peter," John said.

"Yep, that'll buy us just enough whiskey to last us a week, Mister Peter!" James hollered.

The Moores laughed as they walked back to their horse. They still thought the whole day was one big joke.

Peter watched the Moores ride away. He just shook his head in disgust. "*Mister Peter*," he scoffed.

Peter was again embarrassed to turn in such a small load of fish to Mr. Milton. It was nearly closing time and most of his help had gone home.

"Somebody said they saw the Moore boys on your boat," Mr. Milton said. He looked over the fish Peter had caught. "You'd be better off hiring a couple of donkeys."

Peter laughed.

"Yes sir, I'm just about ready to do that."

<><><><>

Later that evening Peter went to Robert Potter's house to give him the money that he owed to the Moores.

"Robert, I'd give them the money myself, but I don't think I could stand another minute of them two."

"Didn't work out, huh?" Potter asked naively.

"*Work?* No, they didn't. Those two men are the laziest, dumbest, childish people I've ever met."

"I suppose that's why my daddy says the Moores are a couple of overgrowed boys."

Potter thought for a moment.

"Hey, my cousin Gerald ain't doin' much work for his pa right now so I'll send him over tomorrow at sunup."

Peter sighed heavily.

"Might as well. He can't be any worse than the Moores."

Much to Peter's surprise, Robert's cousin was waiting at the dock just before sunrise.

Gerald was about fifteen and had a lot of knowledge about ships and their equipment. In fact, it was Gerald's father who made the fishing nets for The *Free Spirit II.*

Unlike the Moores, Gerald never complained about the heat or how hard the work was. Gerald really said nothing unless Peter spoke first. Gerald was not very coordinated and lacked strength, but he did a good job. Peter was not at all embarrassed when he turned in his catch to Mr. Milton.

After they finished, Peter dropped off Gerald at a dock near his house.

"You did a pretty decent job today," Peter said. He tied the Free Spirit II to their dock. "Just be at my dock again tomorrow at sunrise."

"I'm sorry, but I can't work for you anymore, Peter."

"Aw, you can't mean it. The first couple days are always the hardest. Gerald, you did a *good* job out there today."

Peter could not understand why Gerald would want to quit since he never showed any signs of exhaustion.

"Like I said, I just can't do this kind of work."

Gerald climbed onto the pier.

"Well, I'll pay you as soon as I can."

Gerald nodded and began walking away.

"Just spread the word around that I'll be needing some help," Peter called after him. "I don't think my partner will be coming back from Savannah."

Peter was back to where he started at the beginning of the week. He decided to wait a couple of months before writing to Andrew. If he did not hear back from him he would sail to Savannah to meet with him. He also decided to take some time off until he found someone to help him.

Chapter 12 Red

The next morning Peter rode over to Gerald Potter's house to pay him for his work. Mrs. Potter answered the door.

"I've come to pay Gerald for his work yesterday," Peter told Mrs. Potter.

"He's gone to town with his father, but I'll be sure he gets his money."

Peter was still curious about why Gerald quit so abruptly.

"Do you think I worked Gerald too hard, Mrs. Potter?"

"Oh no, Mr. Stewart. Gerald said he liked working with you. It's just that Gerald has a problem."

"Problem?" Peter asked skeptically. "He didn't have a problem putting in a full day's work, ma'am."

"It's not like that. You see, Gerald almost drowned when he was twelve. Ever since then he's been afraid of the water."

Now Peter understood why Gerald was so quiet while they were out fishing. Gerald was so afraid of falling overboard that he was never relaxed enough to carry on a conversation.

"He felt terrible about having to quit," Mrs. Potter went on. "Gerald thought that he could beat his fear by working for you. He doesn't like making fishing nets with his father and wanted to do something different. Please don't tell him we talked about this. He's really ashamed of it."

Peter handed Mrs. Potter the money.

"Mrs. Potter, tell Gerald that it was an honor working with him."

Peter slowly started for Brown's store to talk with Robert Potter. His mind was busy thinking about Gerald's fear of the water and who he could get to work for him. Peter's thoughts were suddenly interrupted by a loud thumping sound coming from behind a house he was passing. As he got further down the road he could see that the noise was coming from a young man chopping wood. Peter stopped his horse and watched him for a moment. He had never seen anyone chop wood so fast. Peter rode over to the young man.

"You sure do work hard."

The young man glanced up at Peter as he reached for another piece of wood to chop.

"Just choppin' wood," he answered. "This is the only way I know how to work."

Peter decided to try to hire the teenager.

"My name's Peter Stewart. I'm a fisherman."

"Yeah I know who you are. I'm Jonah Kelly."

"I need a deck hand until my partner comes back from Savannah."

Jonah kept continued to chop wood.

"Would you like the job?"

Jonah finished his pile of wood. He put down his ax and finally looked at Peter.

"I might if you pay me what you paid Gerald Potter and the Moore boys."

"Oh, so you know about them working for me?"

"It's a small town, you know."

"Of course I'll pay you the same." Peter looked around. "I see you raise hogs and chickens. Do you know anything about fishing?"

"I've fished before; just not on a boat."

"Well if you can work all day like you just did chopping that wood we'll bring in more fish than anyone in the entire state. Do you know where I live?"

Jonah smiled a bit and nodded.

"How about I start working for you on Monday morning around 5:00?"

"Hey, 5:30 is good enough for me."

A great burden had been lifted. Peter somehow knew that Jonah would be a reliable replacement for Andrew.

Potter was showing the dentist's wife a clock when Peter walked into Brown's store. She was apprehensive because Mr. Brown was out on an errand and she always purchased from him. After convincing the woman to buy the clock for her husband's office Potter began apologizing to Peter.

"I know the Moore boys and my cousin didn't work out, but I can find you a good deck hand if you give me a few days."

"Aw, don't worry about it anymore, Potter," Peter laughed. "I found me a new deck hand right after I paid your cousin."

"You did?" Potter was discouraged that he was not going to get another try. "Who'd you get? Don't tell me you got one of those kids from church?"

"No. He's young, but he's no kid. I asked a young man over near where your cousin lives. His name is Jonah Kelly."

Potter nodded.

"That *mulatto* boy?" Potter questioned. "His mother cleans rooms at the hotel. They made me help her so many times when I worked there."

"I don't care what he looks like 'cause he works like I do."

That afternoon Brown came over to put a couple of crates in the warehouse. Peter was glad Brown was there because he had not seen him since the church dinner.

"Good to see you, Brown. I came by the store earlier, but you were not there."

"Oh, I apologize for that. I was meeting with the dentist. He thinks I may need to have a tooth pulled."

"Really? Potter just sold his wife that clock that came from London. I guess the dentist will be getting some of his money back."

Brown and Peter shared a laugh.

"How is the fishing business without Andrew?"

"It's been terrible. I've gone through four deckhands including that new dog we got, but come

Monday I'm getting a new deck hand. I can't wait to get back to some real work."

"Splendid. Splendid. You know...*good Lord, Andrew*. I'm so pleased you mentioned his name to spur my memory." Brown quickly reached into his shirt pocket. "I almost forgot to give you this letter. Please forgive me for my forgetfulness."

He handed the letter to Peter.

"My brother Henry sent me some of my merchandise that was accidentally delivered to his shop. He included this letter for you. It's from Andrew."

"*Andrew*? Peter asked excitedly.

"Yes. It seems Andrew came by Henry's shop and asked that he deliver the letter at his convenience."

"Oh, good. Sounds like he's feeling better if he did that."

Peter gestured for Brown to sit down as he read the brief letter. Brown understood by Peter's facial expressions that the letter contained no pleasing news.

"Is Andrew going to return anytime soon?"

Peter put the letter down and shook his head.

"No. Ole Andrew says he asked Emily to marry him. He's gonna become an overseer at her family's plantation. He gave the farm to the Lumley's."

"Good Lord, man. What will you do now?"

"Well, if this new man does a good job and wants to be a fisherman then he'll be my new partner."

Brown patted Peter on the shoulder.

"It is like I said. Some things are meant to be. I know you wanted to keep the business in the family, but perhaps this is Providence's will."

"Yes sir, I know, Brown. It's a bit disappointing, but Andrew's my cousin and he's his own man like me. I've got to let him live his life the way he wants to. He's gonna be an overseer. You know what that means? He's gonna be in charge of some slaves who work the fields. I can't say that I like that, but he's also my cousin. I think Andrew and I may not see eye to eye on that."

Brown stayed for supper and later had a relaxing conversation with Mrs. Stewart and Peter.

Peter was glad to have Mr. Brown as his neighbor and friend. Mr. Brown had, in a way, filled the place of Grandpa. He was a person Peter could rely upon for advice, or just plain conversation.

Jonah showed up for work on Monday just like he promised. Peter decided not to tell him about the partnership until he saw that Jonah was committed to the job.

Peter spent almost an hour teaching Jonah everything he would have to know about working on a fishing boat. It did not take Jonah very long to get the hang of things. Jonah worked so hard that he and Peter finished a full hour early. Peter was able to take a leisurely course to Mr. Milton's. They proudly passed by the rest of the fishermen still trying to fill their holds.

Peter and Jonah had been so busy while they were out fishing that they had little time for conversation. Since they finished early, Peter took the time to get to know Jonah better.

"What do you think of this fishing business, Jonah?"

Jonah grinned a bit.

"You don't have to call me Jonah. They call me Red at home. I know it doesn't look it, but my hair used to be more red than it is now."

"All right, for now on I'll call you Red. Now really, do you think you will like this job?"

"I like it fine. I already heard that you're probably one of the best fishermen in town, and now that I've seen it, I believe it. I just hope you can pay me what you paid Gerald Potter."

For the first time Peter was disappointed in Red.

"Maybe other people have shortchanged you, but I'm tellin' you, I'll pay you what I'd pay any deck hand."

"I'm sorry. I just need all the money I can get." Red became melancholy. "My Daddy's been sick for a month now and can't work. Momma cleans rooms at the hotel and my sister works as a nanny for judge, but all of us can't live right on what they make."

"You just keep working like you did today and believe me you'll have more money than anyone around here would pay you."

Red smiled.

"I believe you now, Peter. You're a good man."

Red noticed Peter's necklace as Peter bent over to pick up a mooring rope for the boat.

"What you got under your shirt? Some kind of necklace?"

Peter took out his lion's claw necklace. He unfastened it and handed it to Red.

Red studied the claw on the necklace.

"What's this from; some kind of panther?"

"That claw came off a lion all the way from Africa."

"Really?"

"Yep. A man from Africa gave me the necklace. He works on a ship for the company that Mr. Brown gets his supplies from. His name is John, but he doesn't have a last name. We became friends on the way here from England."

Red handed the necklace back to Peter.

"His captain said that they would be sailing here from England someday so maybe you'll get to meet him."

<><><><>

During the next two weeks Red proved to be a valuable deck hand. He worked even harder than Andrew and quickly learned to sail the *Free Spirit II*. On the average day he and Red caught more fish than

he and Andrew did on their best day. The days seemed
to pass by more quickly. Red had the dedication to his
job so Peter decided to offer him the opportunity to be
his permanent partner. Red was surprised at first, but
graciously accepted the partnership. There was
camaraderie with Red much like Andrew. Peter was
pleased to find that he and Red thought alike and got
along well. Red joined Peter and his friends in their
card games at the town meeting hall. Peter's friends
were a bit reluctant at first, but soon accepted Red.
Peter got to know Red's parents and his sister Ellen.
Peter often invited Red's family over for supper. Peter's
mother found out that Red's mother was good at
sewing so she offered her a partnership in her sewing
business. Peter was relieved that his life had returned
to a more normal pace. In the back of his mind he
wondered how long it would last.

Chapter 13 The Visitor

One time after returning from fishing Red and Peter noticed Robert Potter was waiting for them on the front porch. He ran out to the pier and handed Peter a letter. It was marked *Margaret and Peter Stewart* and had *England* stamped on it. Peter realized the letter might be from the man who claimed to be his father. He said goodbye to Red and thanked Robert for bringing him the letter. Peter rushed to the house to find his mother so he could show her the letter. Mrs. Stewart had just finished cooking supper and was about to set the table. Peter had his mother sit with him while he opened the letter. As Peter expected, the letter was from Mr. Monroe. Peter read the letter aloud to his mother.

Dear Margaret and Peter,

I hope this letter finds you both in good health and spirits. Peter, I trust you had a safe journey from England. Words cannot express how thrilled I was to see what a fine man you have become.

My thoughts are constantly occupied with the hope of seeing you both. Margaret, I am the lowest of humans for what I have done to you and our son. I deserve nothing but disgust. My love for the both of you has never ceased and never wavered.

I have made arrangements to travel to Georgia. By the time you receive this letter I shall be under way on my journey home. The time has come to face my responsibilities and shed this false identity.

I am John Stewart.

With the deepest love possible,
John

Peter handed Mother the letter to gauge her opinion. Mrs. Stewart retrieved the previous letter from Monroe and compared the handwriting.

"It's the same handwriting all right." She shook her head and had a disgusted look on her face. "I hope he does come to town. I want to settle this once and for all."

Peter knew that if anyone was strong enough to handle such a situation it was his mother. It was, in fact, her brand of attitude and determination that Peter used in dealing with difficult situations.

"I can't wait for you to meet this man either," Peter said in agreement. "I'd also like to get this settled."

<><><><>

It was not two days later when Red and Peter were again met by Potter as they docked the *Free Spirit II*. Potter kept rubbing his hands together. It was obvious that he was extremely nervous. He motioned for Peter to come closer before he said anything. He was afraid that Red would overhear him. Red noticed Potter's secrecy and abruptly left for home. Peter was irritated with Potter.

"Why didn't you just tell me what you got to say with Red here? He's my partner and my friend and I trust him with anything you have to tell me."

"Oh not this you don't." He gestured for Peter to sit down on the edge of the pier. "A stranger came into town today. He come by the store and was askin' me all sorts of questions about you and your mother, but I acted like I didn't know who you were."

Peter's heart started to race, but he remained calm in his outward appearance. Potter continued.

"He said his name was Monroe. He's staying down at the hotel. Who is this man? Are you in trouble or something?"

Peter tried to seem uninterested.

"Mr. Monroe? He's just someone who works for the company that supplies Mr. Brown's store. I met him while I was in England. Brown knows him too. I'll bet he talked with Mr. Brown, didn't he?"

"He sure did. They talked for an hour or so." Potter relaxed a bit. He seemed to be satisfied with the explanation. Just as he was about to climb on his horse and leave he had a thought. "I just thought it was odd for a stranger from England to be asking questions about you. There is one thing I still don't understand. If you and Mr. Brown met him in England then why was he asking me questions about your mother?"

Peter thought for a quick answer.

"I guess you'll have to ask Mr. Monroe that the next time you see him."

Peter went inside and found his mother.

"What in the world was Robert Potter doing standing on our pier?" she asked. "He must of been out there an hour and a half."

Peter put a piece of kindling in the stove and looked in a couple of the pots to see what his mother had been cooking.

"Uh, Robert was waiting for me. He says that Mr. Monroe, or whoever he is, checked into the hotel this afternoon."

"He's *here* already?" Mrs. Stewart asked. "You just got the letter from him...well, what are you going to do?"

"I think I'll let him come to me. If he's a liar I don't want him thinking I'm anxious or anything."

Mrs. Stewart nodded in agreement.

"I want to get a good look at him, but I don't want him seeing me first. I think I'll get Mrs. Holloway to get a real close look at him first. Her husband was John's closest friend. If anybody around here remembers what John Stewart looks like its Prudence Holloway.

A few minutes later someone knocked on their front door. Peter and his mother looked at one another expecting the other to go answer the door. After they heard louder knocking Peter went and answered the door. It was Brown.

"Pardon me for the intrusion Peter, but did Robert Potter inform you about the visitor we had today?"

Peter gestured for Brown to come inside.

"Potter told me all right. Is it the same man you saw on the docks in Liverpool?'

"Oh yes it is the same man indeed. He's still calling himself Mr. Monroe, you know."

Mrs. Stewart came in to say hello to Brown.

"Why don't you stay for supper, Richard?"

"Oh no, Mrs. Stewart; I wouldn't dare impose."

"I'll have none of that. You will stay and eat with us."

The three of them discussed Mr. Monroe over dinner.

"Potter said Mr. Monroe was asking him questions about us. Did he do the same with you?" Peter questioned.

"No, not at all. We simply discussed business. He said my brother Henry would be here any day with a new shipment from England. He asked me if my shipments had been arriving on time and in good condition. I assumed he might be here to check on the franchises."

"Richard, I'd like to get Mrs. Holloway to look at this Mr. Monroe and see if he really is John Stewart," Mrs. Stewart said bluntly. "Is there some way to arrange a meeting or something?"

Brown looked to the ceiling in thought.

"Perhaps Mrs. Holloway could pretend to be browsing through my store whilst Mr. Monroe is there. You see, I'm sure that I could invite him there to look over my inventory in my small storeroom, or such a matter." Brown looked at Peter then Mrs. Stewart and smiled. "Yes, that would work beautifully. Have Mrs. Holloway drop by the store around 9:30 tomorrow. I'll have Robert Potter retrieve Mr. Monroe and we shall let Mrs. Holloway determine this man's identity." Brown looked serious. "I must say that I have grown quite weary of not knowing if this man is an impostor or not. I just can not imagine the strain this has been on the both of you."

Peter could not sleep that night. He lie awake in his bed with his mind racing with thoughts. He wondered if his mother was doing the same.

"Mother, are you asleep?" he called out to her.

"Not hardly, son," she answered immediately from her bedroom. "I've just been thinking about what I'll say when I see him."

"I can't stop thinking about it either. I just wonder what's going to happen. I wonder where all this is headed? I mean you could have gotten remarried. Can you imagine how that would be?"

"God only knows. You just go about your day tomorrow and go fishing with Red like always. That will take your mind off of things. Try and get some rest now, son."

Early the next morning, Mrs. Stewart went to Mrs. Holloway's house to let her know about Mr. Monroe and his claims. Mrs. Holloway was more than willing to help identify whether Monroe was really John Stewart.

At 9:00 Mr. Brown sent Potter over to the hotel to invite Mr. Monroe to visit with him at his store.

Meanwhile, Peter wished he could be at Brown's store to see Mrs. Holloway identify Mr. Monroe as an impostor or his own father. Red had suggested that they not work, but Peter had hoped the fishing would take his mind off the whole matter.

"I should have stayed home today, Red," Peter remarked. "We've been out here three hours and I still can't get my mind off the whole thing."

Red tried to console Peter. "Don't worry about it. Potter's there and so is Mr. Brown. They can tell you about it. Besides, Mrs. Holloway is the one who knows what your father looks like. She remembers him better than you do. Just ask her about it after we get back."

"Alright, I'll stay out of the way, but I want to quit a couple hours early today. I won't be able to wait."

Mrs. Holloway arrived ten minutes after Mr. Monroe. Brown had been worried that Monroe would leave before Mrs. Holloway arrived. He had already showed Mr. Monroe all of the merchandise he had in the back of his store.

Mrs. Holloway pretended to look at some curtains while she took several glances at Mr. Monroe standing in the doorway to the storeroom. He had on a frock coat and was wiping the sweat off his forehead. Mrs. Holloway was not certain who the man was from her vantage point so she took the curtains over to Brown and asked him the origin of the material. Mr. Monroe glanced at her and nodded hello. He suddenly turned and looked at her again. His eyes widened. She could tell from his reaction that he recognized her. From this distance Mrs. Holloway took a long look at Monroe's face. She quickly put the curtains in Potter's arms and said goodbye to Brown as she walked out the door. Brown carefully watched Mr. Monroe. He stared at Mrs. Holloway as she walked out the store and down the street. Brown noticed the perplexed expression on Mr. Monroe's face.

"Is anything the matter, Mr. Monroe?"

Monroe walked towards the windows and looked down the street. It was obvious that he was halfway lost in thought.

"I know that lady. That's Prudence Holloway."

Brown raised his eyebrows in astonishment.

"You're quite right. You say you *know* this woman?"

Mr. Monroe continued to stare out the window.

"I know her from a long time ago."

Mr. Monroe excused himself and walked back to the hotel.

Like Peter, Mrs. Stewart had also wished she could have been at Brown's store. She could not wait to hear the news from Mrs. Holloway. She waited for her on the front porch. Mrs. Stewart was elated to see her walking briskly up the road to her house. Mrs. Holloway was nearly out of breath from walking so fast.

"I *saw* him Margaret. I got a *good* look at the man."

Mrs. Stewart had Mrs. Holloway sit down next to her. She tried not to let Mrs. Holloway know just how anxious she was.

"You sure you got a *real* good look at him?

Mrs. Holloway caught her breath.

"Oh yes. I was not five feet away from him. It's definitely him, Margaret. That man is John Stewart all right. He's got some silver hairs and a few wrinkles, and he's a lot paler and thinner, but I'd know him anywhere." She put her hand on Mrs. Stewart's arm. "And Margaret, I think he knew it was me, too."

Mrs. Stewart felt strange. A part of her had been hoping that Mr. Monroe would be some sick impostor and another part of her was excited about her husband being alive. But now that she knew the truth it was hard for her to accept the fact that her own husband had really abandoned his wife and child. Mrs. Holloway stayed with her and they talked the rest of the morning.

Peter could not stand it any longer and was easily persuaded by Red to call it an early day.

"I'll be glad when this whole thing gets taken care of," Peter remarked in disgust. "I haven't had enough full weeks of work since I got back from England because I keep taking days off. Mr. Milton is probably beginning to think I've lost interest in the fishing business." Peter laughed and shook his head.

"You know, sometimes I just wish things would be like they were before I left for England. Look at all the grief it's causing my mother and me."

Peter docked the *Free Spirit II* at Mr. Milton's and he and Red unloaded their haul. After sailing home and tying up the boat at Peter's dock, Red wished him good luck.

Peter found his mother sitting on the back porch petting Shark. She seemed lost in thought because she never answered Peter when he called to her. She stared off in the distance at nothing in particular. Peter sat down next to her and petted Shark as well.

"Oh, hello, son," she said.

Peter realized that Mrs. Holloway had told his mother that she had seen his father.

"Do you trust Mrs. Holloway's judgment, Mother?"

"*Yes Peter.* I trust her." She put her face in her hands and sighed. "Prudence said it was him and I believe her. It doesn't matter because Richard Brown just came by and told me that *he* recognized Mrs. Holloway without being introduced. He even said her name."

"Well, did he tell anyone who he really is?"

"No. Richard said he left the store after Mrs. Holloway walked out."

Now that Peter knew that Mr. Monroe was indeed his father he was especially curious about the man.

"There must be others in town that will recognize him. What will we tell them?"

"Tell them nothing." She beat her fist against her thigh several times. "*He* did this; not us. Let *him* explain it to them. If I know Prudence she'll let the whole town know he's here anyway."

She got up and walked into the house.

Mrs. Stewart began cleaning furiously the rest of the afternoon. Peter decided to help his mother out by fixing supper for them.

Peter and his mother had very little conversation over supper. It was obvious to Peter that she was thinking about how her husband let her believe that he had died at sea. Peter himself was flooded with thoughts of John Stewart. He had thought he would be angered if Mr. Monroe turned out to be his father. Peter was, instead, a bit excited about him being alive and in town. Perhaps it was because he was too young to remember his father that he held no personal grudge. Peter was, however, confused about what his father had done to his mother some sixteen years ago. Peter knew that he probably would not find Island Unknown when he left to find it four years ago, but he was willing to accept the ridicule and humiliation that he would have gotten from Leech Myers and others in town. He did not understand why his father could not have done that.

Peter had just finished washing the dishes when there was a knock at the front door. They were not used to having visitors after supper so Peter looked out the window to see who it was. He expected to see Brown, Robert Potter or his friend Red, but was shocked to see who it was. Peter looked back at his mother who had also come into the parlor to answer the door.

"Well, who is it, son?"

"It's *him*," Peter whispered.

Just then Peter realized he was living through the dream he kept having on the way back from England. Mrs. Stewart stepped closer to the door. She untied her apron and fixed her hair with her fingers.

"Open the door, Peter."

Peter slowly opened the door. Right away Peter noticed the mole near the man's right ear just as his mother had described.

Mrs. Stewart motioned for her son to let John Stewart come inside.

He glanced at Peter and smiled. He then trained his eyes on Peter's mother. He never once looked around the room to see how things had changed in the last sixteen years.

"Hello Margaret."

Peter saw an intense look in his mother's eyes as she returned John's greeting with a cautious nod. All doubt was now erased in Peter's mind. This man was his father.

"When did you give me up for dead?"

"Many years ago," Margaret replied. "*Many* years ago."

John turned to Peter and smiled at him.

"Now do you believe that I'm your father?"

Peter was caught off guard. He had no answer.

"I knew you didn't quite believe me when we talked in Liverpool. I can't blame you for being cautious."

He again turned to Peter's mother.

"Could I please talk with your mother alone?"

Peter looked at his mother for confirmation.

"You wait outside, son."

John patted Peter on the back as he brushed past him on the way to the porch.

John took a seat and Margaret sat across the room from him. He finally stood up and walked around the parlor trying to remember what it looked like when he left. He stopped where Margaret's sewing station was. He picked up one of the dresses Margaret was working on.

"It's been just over sixteen years since I was in this house. Your sewing is incredible."

Margaret was not really in the mood for small talk.

"Why have you come back?"

John did not answer the question.

"I thought you would start crying, or hit me when you saw me, Margaret."

"Well I'm glad that I am handling the situation well. I'm not the same woman you knew sixteen years ago. You're obviously not the same man that I married. Why have you come back *now*?"

John sighed heavily.

"I think about you and Peter every day. I've got no family in England. I don't know if Peter or Richard Brown told you, but I'm half owner of the Carey Company and have lots of wealth, but I know now that the greatest wealth of all is a family." John looked Margaret in the eye. He was almost to the point of crying. "I want to be a father again. I want to have contact with Peter and just be his *father*." His chin trembled.

Margaret was still in control of her emotions though it was difficult. She did feel like crying, and at the same time, she felt like hitting John for what he did to her and Peter.

"You'll have to take up that matter with Peter. That's between you and him since he's an adult." Margaret knew she could not let John leave without hearing how she felt. "I begged all our friends not to tell their children what really happened to you so they wouldn't tease Peter when he was a boy. You know, Peter grew up idolizing you. He thought that you were the bravest man who ever lived. It's plain to see that Peter is the only Stewart alive who's really brave."

John said nothing. He expected to hear the consequences of his actions.

"When Peter was fifteen that boy even went and found Island Unknown just to be like his father."

A flash of astonishment went across John's face.

"I let him go even though it was the hardest thing I ever did. That boy just had to try and find that island for Grandpa and for you. I let him go, but you see, I *knew* he would come back and face life square on even if he failed."

Margaret excused herself from the room. She was finished. John sat there a moment and then walked outside. He noticed Peter sitting out on the pier watching the sun set. He walked down the pier and looked over Peter's boat.

"Your boat looks a great deal like my old one. I can tell that my father made it just by looking at it. What do you call her?"

"Free Spirit II," Peter answered.

Peter was quiet. He had always wished that his father were alive so he could talk to him, but now he could not think of much to say. John sat down beside Peter.

"Your mother tells me you *found* Island Unknown?"

Peter nodded.

"Well you must be a real hero in this town. People had been looking for that island for a long time. Long before I was born."

Peter finally spoke up.

"I was kind of hoping to find out what happened to you. That's mostly why I went."

John smiled. He couldn't help but smile when he was around Peter.

"I never could find that island. I'm proud of you for finding it. What did you see on the island, Peter?"

"Well, Grandpa told me you scratched the heading and course to steer under a workbench. When I was out there on the ocean for several days I just about gave up and was ready to turn around when I saw it. Everything Mr. Jenkins said was true. There were reefs all around it and a wrecked galleon. There was also another wrecked ship. When I got on the island I found a shack that some pirates had built from their wrecked ship. One of the pirates left a diary and a map of where their loot was buried. I dug it up and brought it home. I lost some of it when I was swimming back to my boat though."

"Well, your grandpa must have been awful proud of you," John said.

"I can't say if he was or not. He died just before I left."

John frowned.

"What did he die from? Was he in pain when he died?"

"Oh no, he was real tired and all, but no pain. It was his heart I think." Peter tried to reassure him. "He just died in his sleep. He knew he was going to die so he made me promise to find Island Unknown."

"I guess he's buried over in the town cemetery?"

Peter nodded.

"I'll go find him. God, I miss that man. I miss his smile and the things he would say. He could get so excited." John sighed heavily. He stood up and looked back at the house. "I've missed so much of my family's life. If I had been taken away by somebody it would have been easier, but *I'm* the one who did this. I let my pride ruin me and my family's life."

Peter did not try to reassure him this time. He agreed with the man. He finally decided to speak his mind.

"When I was little I remember Grandpa and Mother telling me that you were coming back. I can't imagine how worried they must have been. I still can't understand how you could have left us like that. We had to live on Grandpa's income and then Mother took on sewing. I helped out when I was old enough to work. And all those years I heard nothing but great things about you."

Again, John was on the verge of crying.

"Of course I'm not the man you thought I was. Why, nobody could live up to that kind of a reputation. Your grandpa loved to stretch the facts. I'm sure he had me walking on water." John wiped his eyes. "Looking back on things I can't believe I did something like that. I was a coward back then. I can't live like this a day longer. I just want to be your father again. This time I want to do it right."

Peter himself started choking back tears.

"I want that too, but I don't know if I could call you Father again. Grandpa had to be my father when I was growing up. It's gonna take some time."

A tremendous pressure was released from John. He had been in his own torment for sixteen years. He wiped the tears on his sleeve and regained his composure.

"I've decided to sell my part of the company in England and move to Brunswick. Mrs. Carey, the original owner's wife, died two days after you left Liverpool. She left her half of the company to her nephew. He knows about my past. He's already agreed to buy my half. I plan to open up a textile factory here. You know, you can be my partner if you want. I just had a look at the dress your mother is making. She is very talented. I know many of the ladies back in England would be happy to pay good money for dresses like that. I'm sure many ladies here too."

Peter looked up at his boat.

"I can't speak for Mother, but I'm happy being a fisherman. I do a good job and I've got a great partner to help me." Peter thought about African John, Braganza, and Captain Chester. "What will happen to the people working for your company?"

"Everyone will stay where they are and still have the same wages. The only person leaving is me. Mrs. Carey's nephew has agreed to let Mr. Reece stay on and manage the company. The Browns will still have their franchises. Why do you ask?"

"When I went to England I met a navigator for Captain Gibson named Braganza. He said he hoped to be navigator on the China route. Could you help him? He's really good."

"It is done," John said without hesitation. "I'll mention it to Mr. Reece when I get back to England. Is there anyone else?"

"Captain Chester. He works the route here in America. He wants to captain the Far East routes."

"Then I'll have Mr. Reece make Braganza the navigator for Captain Chester. Is there any one else?"

Peter felt satisfied that Braganza and Chester would receive promotions.

"There is one more man I'd especially like to see get taken care of. He's an African deck hand for Captain Gibson. His name's John, but his friends call him African John." Peter pulled the claw necklace from beneath his shirt. "John gave me this necklace. He's one of the wisest men I ever met."

John leaned over and looked closely at the necklace.

"I've seen those. That's a warrior's necklace. He must of thought a lot of you to give you a lion's claw necklace."

"African John wants to open up a store in America. Can you help him?"

"Well, there are people in England that can help him. They are connected with the antislavery people in the northern states. I could help your friend open a store here, but he'd have too hard of a time because he's from Africa. The north would be better for him. It would still be difficult, but the antislavery people could help him. I'll have your friend, African John, meet with the people in England. I want you to write all this down so I can take that back to England." He put his hand on Peter's shoulder. "Don't worry. I'll see that Mr. Reece takes good care of your friends, Mr. Brown included. The new owner is a good man. Mr. Reece will do anything for me. He and Mrs. Carey's nephew are the only ones in England who know who I really am."

Peter had a lot of things he wanted to tell his father. He wanted to tell him the highlights of his childhood, and at the same time, he wanted to curse him for not being there to see them. Somehow he believed that he would come back from England and live permanently in Brunswick. Then they would have plenty of time to get to know each other and maybe then Peter could begin to understand his father's actions sixteen years ago.

John took out his watch to check the time.

"It's getting late. I best be going since you have to get up so early. Do you still have my old watch?"

"I keep it in the house and wear it to church."

John smiled.

"I thought you or your mother might have thrown it in the ocean by now."

Peter laughed.

"I thought about doing it several times on the way back from England."

John laughed with him. It had been a long time since he laughed.

"You look good with that beard, Peter. I first grew mine when I was your age." He rose to his feet. "The ship will be here soon to unload and I'll board it to Savannah. From there I'll sail with them back to Liverpool. Perhaps these people you want me to help will be part of the crew that comes here."

"Do you know what ship it is?" Peter asked. "Is it The Confidence?"

"Now, that I do not know. Last I heard when I left Liverpool is that the ship would sail in two days and they were sailing straight to Brunswick. So, that should put them here tomorrow or so. You should have seen the crew on the passenger ship that brought me to Charleston. They have much to learn. The little crew I hired to bring me down here from Charleston did twice the work than the ones on that passenger ship." John stood on his feet again. "In the meantime I'm gonna let people in this town see me. I'll tell anybody I run into who I am and what I did to you and your mother." John started to walk down the pier. Peter remained seated. "I tell you, I'm gonna be John

Stewart again. I'll have to earn everyone's respect again, but I'll do it even if it takes the rest of my life."

<><><><>

At breakfast the next morning Peter told his mother everything his father had said to him the night before. She acted like she was skeptical of John's return to Georgia.

Peter went to work and Mrs. Stewart sewed on a dress for the preacher's wife. The morning seemed to breeze by for Peter as he and Red discussed John Stewart.

It was not quite 10:00 a.m. when Mrs. Holloway drove up with her children. She was driving her wagon so fast that her children had a hard time hanging on. Mrs. Stewart had taken a break from her dressmaking and was weeding the front flower bed. She almost had to jump out of the way of the wagon because Mrs. Holloway was in such a hurry.

"Margaret!" Mrs. Holloway yelled. "Do you know what he's *doing*?"

"Do I know what *who* is doing?" a confused Margaret asked.

"That *John Stewart*. He's going all about the town telling people who he is and how he left his family and all. He's asking people if they will let him earn their respect." She took a breath. "Everybody is talking about it. I can't believe you haven't heard."

Margaret did not believe John would actually do it when Peter told her about it. For a brief moment she began to wonder if John Stewart had changed and was sincere about everything he said.

John Stewart had covered just about every business by noon. He saved the preacher for last. After getting directions to the preacher's house John set out to confess to him. Most of the townspeople reacted with shock as John told them his story. Each person was too caught off guard to react negatively towards him. With every confession John felt more and more of his sixteen year burden being lifted. He could not wait to return and start a new life.

As John walked up the path to the preacher's house he noticed an old man tending to a garden near the house. John assumed it was the preacher and started towards him not knowing it was really Leech Myers.

Leech spent his weekdays doing odd jobs for the preacher and the church.

"Afternoon to you preacher," John said in a bold voice.

Leech stopped his hoeing to examine the stranger.

"Preacher's inside the house. I jist work for 'em." Leech stared hard at John trying to figure out where he had seen him before. Much to Leech's surprise, John inadvertently helped jog his memory.

"My name's John Stewart. I used to live here sixteen years ago and..."

"*Stewart?*" Myers interrupted. "John Stewart you say?"

"Why yes sir, that's my name. I..."

"I *knowed* I'd seen ya' before. I heard some people said you came back from the watery grave. You don't know who I am do ya'?"

John looked closely at Mr. Myers' face.

"You do look vaguely familiar."

"Ah, I ain't the same as when I last seen ya'. Does the name Jim Myers mean anything to ya', *Stewart?*"

"Jim Myers?" John thought for a moment. "No sir, I can't remember a Jim Myers."

Mr. Myers stepped closer to John and showed him his famous toothless grin.

"How 'bout *Leech* Myers?"

John pulled away slightly. Memories of rage came back to him as he remembered the repeated tauntings from Myers when he announced that he would find the treasure on Island Unknown.

"I remember you," John said. He tried to conceal all emotion. "My son says that you're a saved man now. You sure look different."

"Your *son* says so? Yeah, I'm saved all right. Are *you*?"

John looked nervously towards the preacher's house.

"I need to talk with the preacher."

"The preacher's asleep. He always sleeps after he eats his noon meal."

John began to start off to another house.

"Now hold on there, Stewart! You knowed I was a diffrent' man the last time you seen me so jist hear me out."

John stopped and faced Mr. Myers.

"Back then I was a *mean* one. I done some things that even the preacher don't know about. I hated jist about everythin' but whiskey. And, oh how I loved *tearin'* folks down to size. Yes sir, I was like the devil himself until your *son*, as you call him, showed me the light by findin' that treasure. Been a long time since a man had stood up to me." Myers pointed the end of the hoe at John's chest. "I tell you I was mean in my time, but I'd *never* of run out on my wife and kid if I had such a family'. I never had me no purty wife like you had and I *hated* ya fer it."

John looked down at his feet in shame.

"That Peter Stewart is more man than you *ever* was. He give a lot of that treasure money to the church and to folks that needs it." Mr. Myers chuckled. "Maybe I'm too old to knock you down flat with this here garden hoe, or maybe not . I jist hope that *son* of yours knocks you down real good. He's sure got more meat on em' working those fishin' nets than you ever had." Myers chuckled again. "Well go on, Stewart. *Git on outta ere' ya coward!*"

John had come back to Georgia expecting to humble himself before his wife and son. Leech Myers was the last person he expected to give him a valuable lesson in humility. After having faced Leech Myers and many of the townspeople, John was now even more committed to trying to start living the truth. He then walked to the cemetery to pay his respects to his father.

Chapter 14 This Isn't Goodbye

Peter was feeling especially happy with his life. Somehow, he knew in his heart that his father would return from England in a couple of months and live in Georgia for good. A part of him secretly wished that his mother would take his father back so they could be a family again, but he would not blame her if she did not.

As Peter and Red docked the Free Spirit II at Mr. Milton's pier they were surprised to see Mr. Milton himself.

"He never comes out to the loading dock," Red noted.

"Yeah, something must have happened."

Mr. Milton caught the mooring rope and tied off their boat.

"Stewart, a word with you in private."

Mr. Milton motioned for him to follow him down the pier a little ways.

"Peter, you might want to sit down for this. I just about fainted when he came in to my office."

"You mean you saw my father?"

"How on earth? Well, I guess he would show up at your house first. I just thought I'd let you know as soon as I could. He came in to tell me he'd been living in England all this time and was too much of a coward to come back after he couldn't find Island Unknown. It was enough of a shock to see a ghost, but to know he did all that. I thought I knew him pretty good back then."

"I'm glad he's facing up to what he did to all of us. Thank you for telling me, Mr. Milton."

As they docked the Free Spirit II back home Peter was a little surprised to see John Stewart waiting for them front of Browns' warehouse. It did not take Red long to figure out who the stranger was.

"That's got to be your daddy standing' there," Red said. He looked again as he tied up the sails. "You two look a whole lot alike."

John waited for them next to Red's horse under a shade tree.

"What do you do with Grandpa's old workshop?" John asked.

"That's where Mr. Brown keeps his large crates of furniture and things like that. I thought about using it for a fish market, but I stayed with fishin'. I just didn't have a use for it myself." Peter turned to Red. "This here's Red Kelly; my partner."

Red and John Stewart shook hands.

"You really going to make a factory, Mr. Stewart?"

"Just as soon as I get back from England, Red." John looked at Peter. "Of course I'll have to find a place to live first."

Peter glanced over at his house looking for his mother.

"Have you talked with my mother today?"

"No. I figured that I better stay away from her. I want to give her a lot of time. I'll just take things slow and gradual. I can only hope things will change once I move back." John gave a tight smile. "I just came by to tell you I'll drop by later this evening to visit. Maybe it will be easier for your mother if we're all together. I'll take dinner at the hotel and then I'll walk over."

Red saw that John was going to walk back to his hotel.

"Hop on my horse. I can take you back to town a lot faster."

Peter's mother was waiting for him in the parlor. She had her arms folded and she was not smiling.

"I saw him out there talking to you and Red," she said. "What did he want? What did he tell you?"

"He just said that he'd come by later to say goodbye to us."

"*Goodbye?* He just got here and he's already running off again?

"The ship from England will be here soon. He's gonna board it to Savannah and then they go to England. He said he'd come back for good after he sells his business back in England. I told you all that before, Mother."

"Well, I can't see why he has to sneak around here to tell you all that."

It did not take long for Peter to figure things out.

"Sounds like you're mad because he didn't come to the door and talk to you."

"*What?* Whatever gave you a notion like that? I... I just think it's rude is all."

Peter went into the kitchen to wash up for supper.

"Uh, huh. You're mouth says one thing, but your eyes tell another story."

Mrs. Stewart started to set the table. She almost threw the forks on the table and set the plates down so harshly that Peter was afraid she would break them.

"Do you know he *actually* went around the whole town telling folks who he was and how he pretty much ran out on us?"

Peter's eyes lit up and he smiled.

"Mr. Milton said he came by his office. I figured would just talk to people who knew him. He really did it, huh? The *whole* town you say? Looks like he's changing his ways, Mother."

She halfway frowned at Peter.

"The preacher's wife came by earlier to try on the dress I'm making for her. She sad Mr. Myers lit into him and called him a coward. She was afraid Mr. Myers was going to start hitting him with a garden hoe. We'll just wait and see if he's changed all right. Let's see if he comes back from England like he said."

<><><><>

Peter went out on the porch to wait for his father. The sun was just starting to set. Something caught his attention in the corner of his eye and he noticed a large ship coming in from St. Simon's Sound. Peter walked out to his pier for a closer look.

"Oh, I'd love it if that was The Confidence."

The ship sailed on past towards the docks in town. A few minutes later it came back and dropped anchor in the middle of the river. A rowboat was let down and two men started rowing towards Peter's pier. They were measuring the depth of the water.

"Hello!" one of the men yelled to Peter. "Do you know where we could find Richard Brown's warehouse?"

"This is the pier for the warehouse!" Peter yelled back. "Is that The Confidence?"

"Man must be a bloody mind reader," one of the men said to the other.

Just then Peter recognized one of the men in the rowboat.

"Fletch? Is that you?"

"Right you are, Peter. Don't you know your old friend Fletch? We got another deckhand 'ere named John, we do. He wasn't with us last him we sailed. We call 'im Pirate John, but he weren't no actual pirate."

"I didn't know you without your arm in a sling, Fletch."

"Do ya 'ere the funny man makin' cracks about me arm?" Fletch said to Pirate John. "That's a right fine American welcome I get."

Peter and Fletch laughed.

"Alright, I'll let Gibson know she's a good depth to moor up to 'alf the pier she is."

Fletch motioned to the ship to weigh anchor and dock at the pier.

Peter ran and let Brown know his shipment was here. After the ship docked at the pier Brown and his brother Henry hugged and slapped each other on the back. Henry provided news of how their sister Vivian was doing. Brown and Peter were excited to see the crew again. They said hello to Captain Gibson and Braganza. About that time Peter's mother came out of the house to see the ship.

Peter introduced Henry, Captain Gibson and Braganza to his mother. They watched the deckhands unload Brown's part of the shipment to the warehouse. Peter was beginning to think African John was not part of the crew until he saw him and another crewman carrying a large crate. John smiled when he saw Peter. After he unloaded the crate he went to say hello.

"My friend Peter from Brunswick," African John said.

They shook hands and hugged. Peter took out his lion's claw necklace.
"The little kids around here always ask me to show them this." Peter turned to his mother. "John, I would like for you to meet my mother."

"Peter talks about you all the time, sir," Mother said.

"Oh, *sir?* Thank you for that. I liked talking with Peter as we sailed from England. He is my friend. He is a good man."

Captain Gibson walked over to let Brown know that all his shipment was in the warehouse.

"Captain Gibson, we'd like to invite you and Braganza and African John to stay the night in our house," Peter offered.

"Yes, we'd love to have you stay," Mrs. Stewart added. "You men can stay in the room my nephew was using. If you are hungry we still have some cake I baked earlier."

"I appreciate your kind offer. I can't speak for Braganza and African John, but I know most of my men are thirsty for more than water," Gibson said.

"Well, you'd be looking for the Lighthouse Tavern," Peter answered. "Just follow this road. It goes right by the place."

African John and Braganza retrieved their belongings and went inside to have some cake. Henry, Peter and Brown stayed on the porch. Henry talked about his trip over from England. Later, Braganza and African John came out and joined in on the conversation.

Peter's mother stepped out on the porch and motioned for Peter to come inside.   She led him to Andrew's room.

"I hope I didn't offend your friend. The one they call African John. He said he wants to the sleep on the *bare floor*."

"Oh no, Mother. I thought it odd too until he showed me his cabin on the ship. He just never got used to a bed is all."

Peter went back on the porch to visit with everyone. He kept looking down the road towards town for his father. He finally saw him coming up the path to the house.

"Evening everyone," John said as he stepped onto the porch. "I trust the journey from England was safe?"

"For those of you who don't know this is Mr., uh, this is one of the owners of the company," Peter said. His father gave him an accepting nod.

Peter introduced each person to his father.

"Mr. Reece tells me the crew has done an outstanding job," John said. "No merchandise has ever been lost or broken and delivered in good time." He glanced over at Peter. "Mr. Braganza, my son tells me you would be interested in navigating the China route?"

"Yes sir. My brother, Vicente is a navigator on that route and I would be happy to sail to the Far East also."

"It's a lot longer voyage than coming over here," John noted. "Do you have family Mr. Braganza?"

"I do sir. My wife and daughter are in Liverpool."

"It took me many years to learn that family is the most important thing. I wasn't a part of my wife and son's life for many years and it was a big mistake. You'd be apart from your daughter most of the year."

"I am ready. I want to do this while I'm still young. I think I would regret not going to China, sir."

"Well, the good news is we should be getting a new steam ship any day now. They just started building a second one. That will cut the time it normally takes on the Far East route so our crews don't have to be away from family so long. Mr. Braganza, when we get back to Liverpool I want you and your wife to meet with Mr. Reece. Maybe you could try the China route out once and see."

"Don't forget about Captain Chester," Peter reminded his father. "He doesn't have a family."

"Captain Chester said he will meet us in Savannah to take the merchandise north," Henry added.

"We'll see if Chester can get another captain to sail north and he can come with us to Liverpool. I want to make sure Mr. Reece and the new owner gets all this done in writing."

"One last person," Peter put his arm on African John's shoulder. "My good friend here."

"Ah yes," John said. "I know the new owner mentioned wanting to open more franchises. African John, would you be willing to work in one of our stores in England to learn how to run a store?"

African John could not believe what he was hearing. He looked at Peter.

"Sir, you would help me to open a store?" African John asked.

"Mr. Reece mentioned Boston as a location for our next store. There would be people there who can help you. We would send an assistant with you to help you with the store for as long as you need him."

African John was speechless. He started to tear up and wiped his eyes with his shirt sleeve. Peter patted him on the back.

"It's what you've always wanted, my friend," Peter told him.

"Might I speak on behalf of my brother," Richard Brown announced. "Henry and I would be delighted to provide any assistance you should ever need. We would be proud to have you join our little brotherhood of franchise owners in the Carey Company."

"It's not going to be easy," John cautioned. "Even in Boston there will still be people who could cause problems." He walked up to African John and extended his hand. "I'll promise to do my best to help you. I want you to meet with me and Mr. Reece when we get back to England." The two shook hands. "My son thinks a lot of you, Mr. *John*? I think you need a last name."

"Last name?" African John questioned. "He looked at Peter."

"Well not John Peter. That sounds funny. Maybe John Peters?"

"No, not Peter," African John said. "*Brunswick.* I have a good friend there."

"John Brunswick," Richard Brown said loudly. "It has a good sound to it. John Brunswick, *proprietor.*"

"Boston franchise owner, John Brunswick," Henry added.

"I can imagine a lady saying, 'I need to go down to Brunswick's to order some new curtains'," Peter added.

John looked over at Peter and nodded.

"Well, it's all settled. Now, if you excuse me I need to visit with Peter's mother privately before the hour gets too late."

The Browns bid everyone a good night and Braganza and African John went to their room in the house.

Margaret came out on the porch and Peter went out back to feed Shark.

Margaret looked to make sure the Browns were far enough down the road so not to hear their conversation. She checked one more time to make sure Braganza and African John had turned in for the night. She kept up her suspicions of John.

"I know you went around apologizing to my friends and neighbors. I'll have you know that it will take a long time for me to accept your apology."

John sat silent and gazed at Margaret.

"Peter tells me that you're already leaving for England."

"*Already*, Margaret?

"Oh, no you don't." Margaret snapped. "Do you really think I'm just going to take you back with open arms after sixteen years?"

John shrugged his shoulders.

"I just don't see how things could ever be the same," she said.

"I know, Margaret. I told you that I wanted to be near my son, but I also want to be near my wife. We are still legally married. I have only loved you and now that I've seen you again I know that I still love you."

John's eyes began to fill with tears. This time, however, Margaret had tears in her eyes too. She nodded and slowly made her way to the door. She opened it and stood in the doorway.

"*If* you do come back I suppose you can come over for Sunday dinners."

John took her hand.

"I promise you that I'll never leave again. I'm taking care of everything when I go back and I will be in Brunswick till I die."

"Well, when I'm convinced that you've really changed there might be a small chance for us to start over- as friends."

John's face lit up.

"As long as there's even a small chance I'll keep trying to prove myself to you."

John left Margaret and went looking for Peter. He found him out back tending to his dog. Shark started to whine when John approached.

"Hey, he didn't even bark at you. He must've gotten used to you already."

John leaned over and petted Shark on the head.

"You know, I've got *four* dogs at my house in Liverpool. You didn't get to meet them when you were there. I'll bring them with me when I move back." John stood up and took off his jacket. "It's going to be strange living in this warm weather again. I hardly ever have to take off my jacket in England. I certainly won't need a fireplace around here."

Peter motioned for John to follow him to the pier.

"Let's walk out front. It's a lot cooler out front by the water."

"That's another thing I'll have to get used to. I live a good ways from the ocean. I miss the sound of the waves and all the sea birds. Sometimes I go down past all the docks where the open water is and just sit there in the carriage and take it all in. I can't remember the last time I sailed a boat."

"I guess you will have to build the factory you want to start here. I can't think of a building in town that you could use."

"True. I walked all over town and didn't see a building that would work. I did notice a couple of spots down by the docks that would be a good location. I need to find out who owns the land."

"How many people do you think will work in the factory?"

"I've talked with a man back in Liverpool who owns a textile factory. He suggested I begin with no more than fifty. Once the business becomes more profitable I would expand to making clothes. I could use your mother's talents in designing the clothes the workers would sew."

"You could have over a hundred people working for you," Peter said. "Would you use slave labor?"

"*Slaves*? Absolutely not," John snapped. "I know many businesses here do it, but not mine. Never."

"Good. I've been having a hard time with it. My cousin Andrew in Savannah is an overseer at a plantation. I don't think its right to do that to people."

"The plantation next to their farm?" John asked. "I remember it."

Peter looked back at his house to see if his mother was coming out to the pier, but he could see her sitting in the parlor.

"What's going to happen with all of us," Peter asked. "I mean, you're still married to my mother and all."

John gave Peter a reassuring smile.

"There's nothing I wouldn't want more than to be with you and your mother again. The hurt that I've caused your mother is a lot fresher than yours since you can hardly remember me. Perhaps with time we can be a family again. Learn from my mistake when you have a family of your own. Don't ever hurt them like I did." John felt a flood of emotions again so he shook Peter's hand and patted him on the shoulder. "This isn't goodbye. I'll see you in a couple of months or so. We've got a lot of years to make up."

"Maybe you can go with Red and me some time when we fish. See what you think of the boat Grandpa built."

John was too choked up to speak. He just smiled and nodded.

Peter watched his father walk away into the darkness before he headed back to the house. His mother was now in her room so Peter talked to her through the closed door.

"He's leaving morning with the ship, Mother." She did not respond. "I think I'll go out to our pier to say goodbye to him."

That night Peter had another realistic dream. This time he dreamed that his father was living with him and his mother. Peter and his father went out fishing in the *Free Spirit II*. They were laughing and having a good time when suddenly they came upon Island Unknown. As they came closer to it they could see someone on the beach waving to them. Neither Peter, nor his father, could recognize who it was until they heard the person's voice- it was Grandpa. Again, he looked young. Peter and his father looked at each other. They were elated to see Grandpa again. Peter tried to steer closer to the beach, but a large reef prevented them. They could, however, see Grandpa's face clearly now. He had that same grin that they had always remembered.

"Hey there you two!" Grandpa shouted at them. "I love you boys. I love ya'." Grandpa walked out into the water a few feet. "You *found* everything, Peter. You found it all just like your Grandpa asked you to."

Peter and John really did not know what to say. Everything seemed so real that they were stunned.

"Are you alive, Grandpa?" Peter asked.

"Am I alive? Why I'm more alive right now then I *ever* was."

Just then a group of about twenty people stepped out of the thick undergrowth that covered the island. John recognized one of the women in the group.

"That's my mother. That's your grandma, Peter." John began waving to her. "*Mother!* There are all my grandparents too!"

"I'm at peace now boys," Grandpa continued. "Now that you're going back home to your family I can rest easy now, son." Grandpa put his arm around his wife and laughed loudly. "Both you boys found the treasure. We love ya', boys. Don't you forget that now."

The island suddenly disappeared in a fog and Peter awakened. He wondered if his father had the same dream. Peter thought back to the dream he had where he talked with Grandpa in the shack. He told him he still needed to find the real treasure. All along it was his father. Peter was convinced that the dream was a message of approval from Grandpa.

<><><><>

African John and Braganza had already taken their places aboard The Confidence when Peter awakened. He went outside and found that Red was waiting for him on the pier as usual.

"We're gonna get a later start today, Red. I'm gonna stay here to say goodbye to...uh...to my father."

"You mind if I stay here with you?" Red asked.

"Nope. You are my partner and my friend aren't you?"

Red nodded in approval.

"I talked with your father quite a bit yesterday when I gave him a ride to the hotel. My momma and sister want to work for him when he starts that factory. Momma told me if your mother doesn't want to work with your father then she will stay partners with her. My sister says she still wants to work at the factory. Your father said he'd find a place at his factory for my father to work. I think your father really means what he says."

"Ellen wants to work there? Hmm. Maybe we can all talk about it if she comes with your parents for dinner?

"My *sister*? Yeah, I know she'll come for dinner with my parents when I tell you asked about...Wait a minute. Are you sweet on my sister?

Peter shrugged his shoulders and smiled.

"Well I'll be. Now it's all making sense. Momma keeps asking Ellen if she's sweet on you cause she keeps talking about you."

"She *does*?"

"Lord yes. She's always asking how much fish you caught. Like I wasn't even on the boat. She was so worried you wouldn't like the rolls she made last time."

"I told her they were some of the best I've ever had," Peter interjected.

"Don't I know it. All the way home she kept saying, 'Peter said my rolls were some of the best he'd ever eaten'. Daddy got so tired of it he told her, 'Peter Stewart, Peter Stewart. That's all you got to talk about is Peter Stewart?"

"Hmm. Ellen asks about me a lot?"

Red shook his head and sighed.

"For somebody who can spot a school of fish stirring up the water from almost a half a mile away you can't see to good if you know what I mean."

Peter looked down the road to see if he was coming. Then he looked back at the house just to see if his mother might come out.

A few minutes later they noticed Brown and his brother leave the house and start walking down the road.

"Hey there. Here to see your brother off?" Peter asked.

"Yes, but I'm also here to see Mr. John Stewart off. I want him to pass along a good word to the new owner for my brothers."

"I noticed you walk everywhere. When are you going to get a horse Mr. Brown?" Red asked.

"Oh, I suppose I shall when I can afford a proper carriage. I did have a fine pair of horses back in England. I just prefer a carriage to riding."

"I noticed you said Mr. *Stewart* and not Monroe," Peter said. "I guess he confessed to you."

"Oh yes, I believe I may have been the first in town. Sounds as though your father confessed to most of the townspeople as well. I'm told Mr. Myers gave him a bit of a tongue lashing. It has certainly got the whole town talking. Of course it was not at all a surprise to me since you have kept me informed."

Peter did not show any disapproval in his face so Brown continued. "May I ask how your mother is handling this situation."

"My mother? Oh, pretty good to tell you the truth. You know how she is. She says things can't be the same as they used to be, but we just have to wait and see."

Red motioned to Peter to look down the road and he saw his father.

"Well, this is a surprise," John said. "All of you have come to see me off?"

Henry and Richard shook hands with John.

"I shall look forward to having more discussions with you about England upon your return, Mr. Stewart," Richard said.

"I shall enjoy our brief voyage to Savannah, sir," Henry said. "Please remember my brothers when you meet with the new owner. Do have a safe voyage, Mr. Stewart."

"Thank you, kind sirs. Once again, I apologize for disguising my identity to you two."

Richard and Henry hugged and Henry boarded The Confidence.

Red stepped forward and shook John's hand.

"I can't believe how much you and Peter look alike."

John laughed.

"You just keep catching a lot of fish, Red. I'll see you in a couple of months."

Red went to get his horse.

"Mr. Brown, we best get going? Hop on and I can take you."

Brown looked at Red for a second and then realized his intentions.

"*Oh.* Yes, you're quite right, Mr. Kelley. I must prepare to open my store."

Red frowned.

"I keep telling you; call me *Red*."

"And *you* can call me Brown."

Peter and John laughed at Red and Brown as they rode away.

"I'm sure glad you came out here to see me off, Peter. This means a lot to me."

Peter nodded and looked down at his shoes.

"Well, the quicker I leave, the quicker I can get back here where I belong."

John and Peter shook hands and slapped each other on the back. Peter then reached around his neck and took off his lion's claw necklace.

"This necklace means a lot to me. I'm not giving it to you. I want you to hold onto it for awhile. It'll give you good luck." Peter put the necklace on his father. "Don't let me down again."

He watched his father walk over the gangplank and Fletch took his father's bag down to his quarters. John took a place on deck and watched the crew unmoor the ship. Braganza and African John came on deck and waved to Peter as the ship slowly pulled away from the pier.

Just as the ship started to turn towards the river Peter noticed his mother coming down the pier. John was busy talking with Braganza and African John and did not notice her until she was already standing next to Peter. They could see that he was smiling. Peter waved to his father. He looked over at Mother and she smirked. She hesitated and then also waved. Peter' father returned their waves enthusiastically.

"I was hoping you might come out here," Peter told his mother.

"Now, don't start on me again, son," she said with a sly grin.

They watched the ship as it slowly moved down the river towards the ocean.

"He's coming back this time, you know," Peter said.

Mother nodded and almost started to cry.

"I never stopped hoping he would."

I had the opportunity to visit the light station at Tybee Island, Georgia that is mentioned in the book.

Thank you for purchasing my story. Please do me a favor and leave your honest review of my book on the website you ordered it from. Speaking of websites; check out mine for other stories I have written and what I'm currently working on. henickebooks.com

From my imagination to yours,

Gary Henicke

www.ingramcontent.com/pod-product-compliance
Lightning Source LLC
Chambersburg PA
CBHW030616130626
46552CB00002B/585